ACT OF LOVE

I0592791

Paris Tyler

Love Swan
Books

Post Office Box 401170
San Francisco, CA 94140

Paris Tyler/Love Swan Books
PO Box 401170
San Francisco, CA 94140
www.loveswanbooks.com

Publisher's Note: This is a work of fiction. Names, characters, places, and incidents are a product of the author's imagination. Locales and public names are sometimes used for atmospheric purposes. Any resemblance to actual people, living or dead, or to businesses, companies, events, institutions, or locales is completely coincidental.

Cover Artwork by Sam Mayle © 2019
Book Layout © 2016 BookDesignTemplates.com

Act of Love/ Paris Tyler. -- 1st ed.
ISBN 978-0-9637683-3-9

To the best editor an author could have. A big thank you to RC Weldon for her invaluable help getting this book to publication.

And a special thank you to BJ whose place in my heart reminds me every day that romantic love is both real and magical.

CHAPTER ONE

The deep throbbing bass of loud house music amplified throughout Podium and colorful flashing lights created a frenetic energy that encouraged everyone in attendance to dance. Cleo Martin could feel the vibrations as she moved atop her sturdy column. She was one of a dozen girls perched atop pedestals that were spaced throughout the large dance floor that inspired the Podium nightclub name. Dressed in a black leather vest, biker shorts with fishnet stockings and Doc Martens boots, Cleo was able to move freely on the dance top that was five feet in diameter. It was still early evening by clubbing standards and the dance floor was starting to fill with the Los Angeles crowd who were there to see and be seen.

"Hey, doll, you wanna come over to my place and move like that for me?"

Cleo was used to the come-on lines and she ignored the man four feet below her and his slurred heckling. She avoided making eye-contact that would only encourage the stranger and swiveled on the pedestal as she danced. She searched the crowd for Rock so she could signal the intimidating bouncer if things took a more unpleasant turn.

She scanned the other people dancing around her podium making a quick mental note about the drunk. He wouldn't be a problem.

❦

Drake picked up two drinks from the bar and maneuvered through the crowd to find Randy. He wasn't sure where the other man was but if he knew anything about his client he was likely trolling for women. He scanned the room, looking at the gyrating people on the dance floor not really expecting to see Randy there. He admittedly didn't know his client well, but given his paunch and propensity for drinking he doubted the other man danced much. Randy's main goal for coming to Podium was to feel like a big-shot in a town filled with people wanting to make their mark.

There were a variety of podiums spaced around the dance floor and Drake maneuvered around them, scanning the crowd for Randy. In front of him, a blonde woman dancing on one of the pedestals, caught his eye. Black fishnet stockings covered shapely legs, toned from her nightly workout. Her energy added to her beauty. She was obviously having fun as she danced above the crowd. Drake admired her carefree abandon as she moved. The flashing lights and darkly lit room could be playing tricks on him. In a town full of women who took pains to optimize their looks it seemed unlikely that this one could be as beautiful as she appeared. She was sexy and playful while dancing freely. It took a few seconds to regain his composure after gawking like a teenager. Normally he had complete control over his life and libido. He looked again at the blonde and convinced himself the club lights were playing tricks on him.

Drake spotted Randy seconds later standing in front of the young woman's pedestal. Apparently he wasn't the only one drawn towards this dancer. It'd been two years since his disastrous relationship with Gabriella and swearing off women to focus on his work. *Maybe it was time to reconsider his self-imposed sabbatical from dating?* He pushed the thought away as he re-reminded himself he had a client to entertain.

Randy had already consumed a few drinks, so it shouldn't have surprised him to find him heckling the blonde as he approached. Didn't Randy know the meaning of respect? Possessiveness flared inside him and he fought the urge to push Randy aside and tell him to leave her alone. *Yup. She really had reduced him to a gawking teenager. So much for being a mature thirty-two year old.*

As he got closer to the pedestal he realized his first impression had been very accurate. She was beautiful. She definitely could stop traffic. Nothing was overdone — everything was perfect.

&

Cleo saw a tall man join the drunk below her and offer him one of two drinks. She could see him try to engage the rowdy man in conversation even though the drunk continued to harass her.

"Hey baby, you've got the body — Ever thought about being a stripper?"

Charming.

It was times like these she wished she wore more than the skimpy dancing outfit.

Trying to be subtle in her observation of the

two men, she looked more closely at the one who just arrived. He had dark brown hair and a strong, determined jaw. Because of the distance and dark room with flashing lights, she couldn't tell what color his eyes were. His look was more corporate than the usual patrons of Podium. She was sure she'd never seen him there before. The suit he wore appeared expensive and impeccably tailored. Of course she could be wrong. The lights of the club created an illusion that could fade any impression once removed.

Under different circumstances Cleo was sure the stranger would look very different.

Multi-colored lights flashed and reflected from a large mirrored globe which hung from the center of the room, casting swirling, flickering white lights along the walls of the club. Obviously, the lights were playing tricks on her, making her see a glamorized view of the newcomer she was sure didn't exist.

Cleo noticed the newcomer seemed to have diverted his friend's attention and she began to relax again. She listened to the music and put thoughts of the two men out of her mind as they moved away from her pedestal.

Cleo remembered the first time she'd danced on the podium. It hadn't taken her long to feel comfortable dancing on the confined space and with time she'd gotten more creative. She could match the beat of the music and she guessed that many patrons felt more comfortable taking to the dance floor with the club dancers in place.

She was relieved to see Rock approaching

with Ju-Dee, the dancer that would take her place during her break. The tall brunette had started dancing at the club the same week as Cleo and they'd formed a solid friendship.

Everyone called the large man Rock because he was built like a mountain. No one ever referred to the bouncer by his real name, Henry.

"Ready, honey?" Rock called up to her.

"Yup," Cleo replied as she sat down on the edge of the cylinder. She leaned forward and placed her hands on Rock's shoulders. He hoisted her off the platform and set her delicately onto the hardwood dance floor. Although it was possible to get off the pedestal without any help, it was difficult to be graceful in the process. Cleo appreciated the imposing bouncer's assistance.

Rock playfully pushed Cleo away from the pedestal. "Go! Have a good break." He turned to make sure Ju-Dee was securely settled atop the cylinder before calling over his shoulder, "I'll meet you by the bar in fifteen minutes, Cleo."

It didn't take her long to reach the long counter of the bar. "Hiya, Tony. Have any water for a thirsty girl?"

"You bet, kiddo, just give me a second to finish this order." A minute later, Tony, a flamboyant bartender, gave her a nod as he set a large glass of iced water down in front of her. "For you, kid, no charge."

"I bet you say that to all the water drinkers."

"Only the cute ones," Tony laughed before he moved on to help one of the cocktail waitresses.

The water tasted refreshing and Cleo walked around the club floor, looking at the different people around her. Podium attracted a hip and trendy crowd. Some looked casual in jeans and t-shirts and others were dressed in a variety of the latest fashions. Regardless of how informal someone appeared, Cleo knew most at Podium that evening had spent a great deal of time selecting what to wear. The club scene in Los Angeles was taken very seriously. People were there to make an impression and network in hopes of being seen in a city known for superficial interactions.

"Hey, there you are my blonde beauty. Down from your perch I see." Cleo felt a hand grip her arm and she turned to confront the drunk. Her expression was firm and cold as she looked him directly in the eyes.

"Remove your hand from my arm."

"Oh baby, I love it when you talk rough to me. I bet you're a feisty one. Why don't you show me?"

Cleo could smell the strong aroma of alcohol and knew the man could over-power her. She tried to suppress the panic rising inside her as she looked around for Rock. Although the heckler wasn't exceptionally large, he was drunk and stronger than her.

"If you'll excuse me, I need to be getting back to work," she said in an effort to break free without having a physical struggle.

"Randy."

A clear, deep commanding voice interrupted Cleo's panic. "Randy, this young woman would like to get back to her job. Don't you agree we should let her get on her way?" Cleo locked eyes with the heckler's companion she'd noticed earlier. At close proximity she realized her earlier observations had been very accurate. The man in front of her looked incredible and he filled his expensive suit perfectly.

At close range she could see he had lighter colored eyes than she'd first imagined; a clear hazel color almost translucent in the club lights. He also had laugh lines around his eyes she was sure would deepen if he were to smile. Right now it was hard for her to imagine this powerful man ever laughed or smiled as he firmly intercepted his friend. It was clear he was the alpha dog of the two.

"Just a second, Drake," Randy shrugged off the tall man. "Come on, honey, you have time to join us for a drink, don't you? Isn't your job to make the patrons happy?," he slurred.

Cleo looked from Randy to the tall man in front of her and was surprised to see that he — Drake — looked embarrassed. He'd certainly showed the strength to take control of the situation and extricate Cleo from her current predicament, but she questioned his choice in friends.

Randy was still clutching her arm and yet with Drake intervening, Cleo was sure there wasn't going to be a struggle, however, she continued to scan the crowd for Rock.

"Come on, Randy, we should be going," Drake said to the shorter man. It surprised her that Drake was able to sound so soothing although he was clearly issuing an order. She imagined he was a man most people probably didn't question.

At first Randy hesitated but finally released his grip. "I'll see you later, doll," he said before walking towards the entrance of the club.

Drake watched Randy walk away and then turned toward Cleo. "Sorry to have troubled you. Have a pleasant evening." He pivoted curtly and followed the other man, leaving her with her mouth hanging open, stunned by his formality.

It took a few seconds for her to regain her composure and as she turned to find Rock, she again questioned Drake's choice of friends. She thought it odd since the two men possessed what seemed like polar personalities; one a sloppy drunk and the other a powerhouse in an Italian suit.

Fortunately, the remainder of the evening passed without any other incidents. She was thankful when the club finally closed in the early morning hours. Her acting auditions the previous afternoon had already tapped her energy level and dancing had been the final blow. All she wanted to do was enjoy a luxurious, hot, bubble bath.

"I'll walk out with you, Cleo," Rock called to her as they headed towards the door. "Another day, another dollar, isn't that the saying?" the bouncer joked as he pushed the heavy door open and held it for her to pass through.

"Well, I was hoping for more than a dollar, but I'll take what I can get," Cleo laughingly replied as she waited for Rock to lock the door.

No one, at least no one sober, dared to mess with the powerful bouncer. He was easily six and a half feet tall and Cleo felt like a small doll when she stood next to him. She was sure Rock was at least twice the width of her own body.

She walked towards her dark blue 550cc motorcycle and unlocked one of the side compartments, placed her large, black leather satchel inside, shut the lid and locked it again. Her black bag contained a variety of items; dance clothes for that evening, scripts, and her working bible — her organizer.

"Seems like it was a pretty tame night," Rock assessed the evening.

"Yeah, although one guy was heckling me for a while..."

"Where was I? I would've kicked his sorry ass to the curb." Rock's voice was edged with concern.

"I think you were getting a keg or something. Don't worry, the guy he was with came to the rescue." *Drake had been a knight in shining armor, hadn't he?*, she thought to herself.

"Honey, no one should even get to *think* about harassing you."

"Don't worry, everything worked out fine. Really, Rock, the one guy took control of the situation and took his friend home. I didn't see either one of them for the rest of the night."

"You know, you only have to signal and I'll have any guy giving you problems outside so fast his head will spin." Rock was really sweet the way he looked after all the dancers, not just Cleo.

Rock watched as she finished storing her items and swing her leg over the motorcycle and settle on the leather seat.

"Any more phone calls?"

"Not for a few days. I just hang up when I realize it's the "Creepy Caller." I'm sure he's only looking for a reaction."

"I worry about you."

"Don't. He'll get tired of calling soon because I don't respond."

"Well, keep me posted." Rock unlocked the cab of his white pickup that was parked next to her bike and threw his bag onto the passenger seat. "Any auditions today?"

Cleo held up three fingers. "The last one was a nightmare."

"Something's bound to break soon. You go out on auditions all the time."

"Yeah, but sometimes I feel like I'm getting too old for this. I just thought my life would be different."

"Honey, you're not old — you're twenty-seven. Sounds like the perfect age to me. Besides, you're lucky — you have a great look and high energy level. Not only that, you can act. That's more than most people in this town can say."

Cleo laughed. Right now she didn't have an acting job and it seemed one would elude her for quite some time, especially after her auditions that day. "I have two more auditions tomorrow, so keep your fingers crossed for me."

"Kid, I always keep my fingers crossed for

you," Rock replied genuinely. "You deserve it."

Cleo felt her cheeks warm with Rock's comments. She sometimes felt uncomfortable with compliments, not knowing how to respond in a town where they could be used to manipulate and often felt untruthful. And yet from the bouncer who always spoke his mind she had no reason to question his motives.

"Thanks, Rock, you're great... my biggest fan! She fastened her riding helmet and started her motorcycle. The powerful rumble of the engine shifted to an idle hum and she switched from neutral to first gear. 'I'll see you tomorrow night," she called over the sound of the engine and waved goodbye.

Cleo pulled into traffic and inhaled the scent of salty air, blown inland from the Pacific Ocean. She brought her motorcycle to a stop at a red light on Sunset Boulevard as she neared the Beverly Hills border. She found her thoughts drifting back to the events of the evening and the tall stranger in the expensive suit. *Drake had been an interesting man. Did he live around here?* The way he was dressed could place him in a variety of the upscale neighborhoods in Los Angeles.

Drake had piqued her curiosity. He was so unlike the normal patrons of Podium. *Maybe he lived in Brentwood — full of thirty-something types. Or maybe Bel-Air. He certainly had the formality to fit into the elite community.* The possibilities were limitless. She had fun thinking of the options.

Maybe he lived on The Strand in Redondo

Beach — corporate by week, cruising bikini-clad women on weekends. She didn't know why but she was pretty sure he wasn't the type.

Maybe old money living at home with mommy in Beverly Hills? Hardly. He didn't strike her as a man tied to the apron strings. *Probably a strong family background but certainly his own man.* It was entertaining to ponder the possibilities. She liked contemplating the possible life stories of people and the fun game helped her with her acting as well.

The early morning air was brisk and energizing as she maneuvered her bike down Sunset Boulevard, heading towards her apartment in West Hollywood.

Cleo loved to ride along the Boulevard, winding her way through Sunset Plaza. There were many small boutiques and restaurants along this portion of Sunset and she loved to watch the people gathered there during the day. At the Beverly Hills border, Sunset changed into an exclusive residential drive Cleo also enjoyed but that trek would have to wait for another day. During the early morning the streets were quiet and it was easy to make a left turn off Sunset into the residential area above the strip.

It didn't take long for her to reach the driveway that led to her home. There were two buildings on the lot and she lived in the bungalow behind the main house. Palm trees and flowering shrubs surrounded her home and there was a stained glass window inset in her front door.

She parked her bike, retrieved her black satchel bag and unlocked the door to her apartment. She flipped on the lamp by the front entrance and shrugged her bag off her shoulder, allowing it to drop to the floor. Her answering machine was blinking and she pressed the play button. While the tape rewound she untied her boots, kicking them off her feet and she walked to her bathroom. She turned the white enamel faucets reminiscent of an earlier era to start hot water running for a soothing bath.

Beep. "Cleo, honey, this is Raymond. Call me in the morning and let me know how the auditions went today. And Cleo, I got a call from Bill Meyerson and he's interested in seeing you. Did you hear that, honey? Bill Meyerson! Something about a young girl who lives next door to a family who has some funky secret thing they are hiding. The girl is some type of voyeur... I don't know... I think it's a comedy. I'll have more information for you tomorrow. Call me. Ciao."

Even though she was exhausted, Cleo chuckled. Raymond was her agent and the quintessential embodiment of the Hollywood persona. Cleo thought he was marvelous.

Bill Meyerson. Amazing. He was known for doing good work. Nothing that would ever get nominated for an academy award, but his work always proved successful at the box office.

Beep. "Hi, Cleo. I don't know if you remember me, but this is Larry. I'm a friend of Ju-Dee's. I was wondering if you'd like to get together for a movie sometime. Or dinner. Oh well, you're probably dancing at the club most nights, how about lunch? Give me a call..."

Larry? Who was Larry? Cleo would have to ask Ju-Dee tomorrow night. His voice sounded oddly familiar but she couldn't place it with a face. She absentmindedly scribbled down his number as her messages continued to play.

Beep. "Hi dear, it's your mother. I hope everything's going alright..." Cleo listened as her mother's message filled her in briefly on her parents' activities.

As the tape began to re-wind, Cleo walked back towards the bathroom, slipping out of her clothing as she went, dropping the clothes to the floor. She was naked except for the gold bracelet she always wore. It had been a gift from her grandmother and she never removed it, even to bathe.

She could hardly wait to sink into the luxurious waters and sooth away the tensions of the day.

❦

There were several actresses already sitting and reviewing their lines when Cleo walked towards a table to retrieve her sides; the pages of the scene she was to read.

"I'm Cleo Martin. I'm here for the audition."

The woman behind the table gave Cleo a bland look. "Do you have a photo and resume?"

After she'd handed over a black and white eight by ten photo with her resume printed on the back, the woman gave her several pages from the script, the sides she was to read. Cleo was also given a brief synopsis of the character that provided more insight into the role she was auditioning for than the lines on the few script pages she'd been given.

After slipping into the ladies room to put on a floral skirt over the leggings she'd worn on her motorcycle, Cleo returned to the lobby and sat down to review the pages. The play was a drama and it showed in the scene. *Nothing like a tearjerker to start the day.* She tried to focus on the words in front of her and find the feelings to use in order to convey the character accurately.

She ignored the other actresses around her. It wasn't uncommon for others auditioning to play on any fears they might sense in the others auditioning all in an effort to ruin their competitor's concentration.

She'd learned a long time ago that most of the people auditioning would resort to a variety of methods to strengthen their chances of getting a part. Even casual sounding statements — 'I thought they were looking for a brunette" or "I never would have guessed you were twenty-two" — were said intentionally to create self-doubt. She was immune to these comments and she chose to utilize the time ahead of her to familiarize herself with the character.

"Cleo Martin!" As her name was called she picked up her black bag and headed towards the young man holding the clipboard. "Is that your real name?" he asked as she approached.

"It is," she confirmed with amusement as they walked down the incline towards the stage. She couldn't help but remember the day she and Ju-Dee had laughed together about stage names. "You're lucky, Cleo. You were given a great name at birth. Who wants to see Judy from Nebraska? That's why I made it 'Ju-Dee'."

As Cleo entered the theater she saw several lights set up, illuminating a small section of the black painted stage. Two chairs were placed on the stage, one occupied by a middle aged man who looked bored as he stared vacantly into space. Five people sat in the orchestra section several rows back from the stage, talking quietly.

The young man with the clipboard announced her arrival. "This is Cleo Martin. She's represented by Raymond at The Actors Agency."

"You'll be reading with Robert. Do you have any questions about the character? No? Good." The man who spoke returned his attention to his clipboard as she walked onto the stage. "Whenever you're ready..."

Cleo felt good about her reading. Robert proved to be as bored as he looked and his reading fell flat.

Regardless, she worked on conveying her own perception of the emotions of the character and the end result pleased her.

"Very nice. We'll be in touch with Raymond if we're interested." Cleo couldn't see who was speaking because of the stage lighting.

She gathered up her bag, thanked the group and walked towards the exit. Their reaction had been typical and she knew the decision to cast her in the part could go either way. She was sure Raymond would be calling the director Monday to find out more information if they hadn't heard anything beforehand.

She looked at her watch after she slipped out of her skirt and returned it to her black bag. With half an hour to make it to her next audition, she enjoyed the breeze as she rode her motorcycle through the traffic towards her destination.

Her second audition was at The Stockton Agency located in Westwood. TSA was one of the largest advertising agencies in the city and had a worldwide reputation. It seemed unusual to have a studio at the offices of an ad agency. The Stockton Agency must be very successful to afford the luxury of an on-site studio.

Raymond hadn't given her any information about the commercial but she was sure it was for a national commercial for a large corporation. A commercial would look good on her resume if she got the part and could possibly lead to other work.

She used the ride over to clear her mind and the drama of the scene she'd just read for slipped away.

Her thoughts returned to the evening before. *Would her knight in shining armor return to Podium sometime?* She doubted the club was his normal domain. Pity. She had to be honest. She liked him coming to her rescue. Whoever said chivalry was dead hadn't met Drake. *Too bad she didn't have a last name. He'd be impossible to find.* Not that it mattered — she was sure her fantasies were nothing more than a dream facade that would crumble if she were to spend any time with him. He really seemed too good to be true. Why was she thinking of him anyway? She needed to focus on her auditions.

She felt light and carefree as she pushed open the large glass doors that led into the lobby of the Stockton Tower where the agency was located.

She pulled her skirt out of her black bag and slipped it on over her black leggings as she rode up in the elevator.

"I bet the guards are getting a kick out of this," Cleo laughed as she pulled her sweater down over the top of her skirt and glanced up at the elevator camera discreetly hidden in one corner.

The bell of the elevator rang, announcing her arrival at the twenty-seventh floor. She put her bag over her shoulder and looked down to smooth her clothes one last time before stepping off the elevator.

A starched, white shirt engulfed her vision and the spicy scent of aftershave filled her nostrils as she collided with the man in front of her.

CHAPTER TWO

"Drake!"

Cleo was surprised to find herself use the tall man's name as she tried to step backwards after colliding head-on with the man from the night before. His strong hands were on her waist as he instinctively reached to steady her. The contact felt intimate and she felt a deep, warm blush color her cheeks.

"I'm sorry, I didn't see you." Cleo tried to move away from him and the strong sensuality that enveloped her.

"That's alright. But I must say, you have me at a disadvantage. I only know you as "the dancer from last night" and you're using my name."

"I'm sorry, you startled me. I'm Cleo. Cleo Martin."

"Like Cleopatra? Not a common name, especially for a blonde with blue eyes. Well, Cleo, it's nice to meet you." Drake held out his hand and Cleo reached to take it in her own. As his fingers wrapped around hers in a firm but gentle handshake, Cleo marveled again at his formality. This was a man who exuded both strength and sensuality. A sexy, dangerous combination.

"I'm glad I have the chance to apologize again for last night," Drake said, his eyes locked her gaze.

Cleo could feel her cheeks warm again as she realized she had been standing, holding his hand and staring, for a long time. The warmth from his hand warmed her own and sent a tingling sensation through the rest of her arm.

Last night she'd described him as stunning. Today she realized he was magnetic as well. This type of man was out of her league — Dangerous with a capital "D". Even on a Saturday afternoon he dressed impeccably and expensively in a suit and tie.

"Oh, Drake, I'm glad I found you," a young woman interrupted her quiet observation. "You have a phone call and Rita asked me to track you down."

So it appeared Drake worked for The Stockton Agency. Based on what he was wearing she concluded he must be an account executive trying to impress a boss and move up the chain of command.

"I'll be right there, Mariana," Drake said to the young woman who'd joined them. As he pulled his hand away, he turned back to Cleo. "Are you here for the audition? If so, Mariana can get you set up. Promise me, though, that you won't leave before we have a chance to talk." Without waiting for her reply, he disappeared down the hallway. She noticed he used the same tone as he had the night before with Randy. His words sounded like a question but his tone left no doubt the statement was nothing less than an order.

"Is he always like that?" Cleo asked the young woman in front of her. After she asked the question she wished she could retract her words. She didn't know this woman and she wanted to be professional.

Mariana's reply set her at ease. "Drake? Oh, don't let him bother you. He roars orders like a lion but really he's as tame as a house cat." Mariana let out a bubbly laugh. "But don't tell him I said that — I like getting my paycheck each week."

Cleo liked Mariana instantly. She seemed down to earth, unlike a lot of people she met when she went out on auditions.

"Do you work for The Stockton Agency?" Cleo asked as they walked down the hallway and turned down another.

"I was hired by the agency to be the Production Manager for this commercial. Do you have a photo and resume? Oh, you're with Raymond. Did he tell you we'll need you to shoot for three days starting Wednesday?" Mariana breezed down the hallway and she felt like she was practically running to keep up with her. "Nothing like casting at the last minute!"

"Actually, Raymond hasn't told me very much. I don't even know what product you're promoting."

"Shame on him. I'll have to scold him the next time I talk to him," Mariana laughed. "The product is a combined shampoo and conditioner. The shoot's going to take three days because we're going to show you doing fun, exciting things with the time you save. We're using several locations."

"You make it sound like I already have the job."

"Well, I know what the producer's been looking for and I'll go out on a limb here and say I think you've got it. Most of the other agencies have been sending over people with long, thick, gorgeous hair, but glamour girls aren't approachable. You seem different, like someone the viewer can relate to...and you have great hair."

"You can tell all of this by walking down the hall with me?"

"Actually, I can tell by the way you interacted with Drake. You're approachable. I haven't seen many people get Drake to smile as quickly as you did."

Mariana pushed open the door leading to the production studio and faced Cleo. "I don't want to get your hopes up, but I'd say you're in. Break a leg." Before leaving, she called over to the men in the glass booth along the far wall. "Hey guys, this is Cleo Martin. Be nice."

Cleo waved to the three men and Mariana directed her to a taped spot on the floor in front of a television camera. "We record all the auditions just to see how natural you are in front of a camera. These guys are going to ask you several questions but don't let them scare you."

She took her mark in front of the camera. It didn't intimidate her. She'd lost count of the number of times she'd auditioned on video.

"Can you tell us your name?" a voice echoed from the production room. Cleo stated her name clearly as she looked into the camera. The men already knew it but wanted it at the beginning of the reel. The men asked a variety of questions for approximately ten minutes and then thanked her for her time.

She looked around for Mariana but the other woman was nowhere to be seen. After waving to the men in the booth, she turned towards the door. She found her way back towards the elevators but no one was around.

She didn't know what to do. Drake had said he wanted to talk to her but she had no way of finding him. Maybe the security guard in the lobby could direct her.

She pressed the button to call the elevator as Mariana came running around the corner. "Cleo, Drake wanted me to bring you to his office. Ready?" Mariana fired questions at her as they wound their way along the hallways. "How did it go? Did you feel comfortable? Did they tell you anything?"

Cleo laughed. She felt like she'd known Mariana for years. "Everything seemed to go just fine."

"Great. Here we are." Mariana stopped in front of a single elevator door and entered a code on a security pad. The bell rang and the doors opened to a lush and opulently decorated elevator.

"Where are we going?" Cleo asked.

"Drake's office is on the top floor. This is the express elevator," Mariana replied as she pressed a button inside the elevator.

"Is Drake the account executive on this project?" Cleo asked as they stepped onto the plush carpeting in the elevator.

"I guess you could say he's *THE* account executive on all TSA projects," Mariana answered.

When she saw Cleo's puzzled look, Mariana continued. "I'm sorry. I thought you knew Drake. He's Drake Stockton, the owner of The Stockton Agency."

Cleo felt her legs buckle under her and she was thankful for the railing along the elevator walls. *Drake Stockton?* Cleo guessed somewhere in the back of her mind she knew The Stockton Agency was a privately owned company but she never imagined the owner could be so young. She was sure Drake wasn't much over thirty although he carried himself with the stature of a much older man.

Luckily Cleo regained her composure before the elevator stopped and the doors opened to a large reception area.

Mariana stepped off the elevator first and approached the woman in front of them. "Hi Rita. This is Cleo Martin. Cleo, this is Drake's assistant, Rita. And now that introductions are out of the way, I've got to get back to work. I'll see you both later."

"Mr. Stockton is expecting you. If you'll come this way..." Rita tapped lightly on the door in front of her before opening it and stepping aside to let Cleo pass through. Cleo could feel the door shut behind her as she found herself alone with Drake Stockton.

❧

His office, as impressive as the rest of the building, was laid out in several sections, identified by various pieces of furniture. To the right was an extensive bookcase, wet bar and long table presumably for meetings. To the left, a variety of awards and trophies adorned the walls, along with a fireplace and leather couch, further emphasizing the success of TSA.

A large mahogany desk and a wide window view of the city below loomed before her. Drake pushed himself away from his desk and steadily approached. She tried to stop her heart from pounding so rapidly. Butterflies were swarming inside her and she fought the urge to step backwards. Yup, this was dangerous territory.

"Cleo, come on in. Why don't we sit over here by the fireplace?"

She felt like she knew enough about this man not to be concerned about being alone with him, but she also suspected he was a man used to getting what he wanted. No one would be able to build a company such as TSA without commanding respect and obedience.

Drake motioned towards the brown leather couch in front of the fireplace and Cleo felt herself sink into the rich leather as she sat down. It was wonderful. Normally leather felt cold and stark but this couch was different. She felt cozy and warm as she sank into the cushions.

Drake sat down and looked at her for what seemed like an eternity before he started to speak. "I'm glad I have the opportunity to apologize to you about last night. Randy obviously had too much to drink."

"Why do you hang out with someone you have to apologize for?," Cleo asked without thinking. She wasn't used to having to watch what she said and she was sure she would get herself into trouble if she wasn't careful. "I mean, your choice in friends seems odd." That wasn't much better.

Drake laughed. "Let's just say my friendship with Randy is a professional one, not a personal one. Last night I was entertaining a client, nothing more. He wanted to go to a nightclub and we ended up at Podium."

"Oh. Does that bother you — having to entertain someone you don't like?"

Drake laughed again and the lines around his eyes creased with his smile. "I guess I've never thought about it that way. I've always looked at it as part of the business process, nothing more. It's not about liking someone or not, it's just business."

"You mean you can spend an evening with him and not form an opinion about him?"

"It sounds like you're asking me more about respect than friendship," Drake replied. "Tell me Cleo, when you audition, or when you're working at Podium, do you first form an opinion of someone based on respect or friendship?"

"Well..." There was that tone again. It really sounded like Drake was asking a question but the tone of authority rang through. "I guess friendship does develop after respect although I've never thought of it that way before."

"So, in answer to your question, I think it's possible to have respect for Randy the businessman, without ever forming an opinion about him personally."

He sounded so convincing. Cleo thought

Drake could probably say anything and sound believable. Even if he said jumping off the Empire State Building wouldn't hurt. *Yup, this man could be trouble.*

"Promise me you'll give me a chance to make up for last night." Drake was looking at Cleo intently. "How about having dinner with me tonight?"

"I can't."

"Can't or won't?" Drake asked without missing a beat.

Can't and shouldn't, Cleo thought. Instead she told Drake she was dancing at Podium.

"Of course, I should've remembered dinner would be difficult. Do you dance every night?"

"No, just Wednesday through Saturday," Cleo replied, not sure whether or not she felt comfortable discussing her work schedule with Drake Stockton.

The loud tone of an intercom interrupted their conversation and Drake excused himself as he stood and walked towards his desk. His office was large enough that there was a sizeable distance between the couch Cleo sat on and his desk and Cleo felt isolated as she waited for Drake to return to the couch. From the tone of his voice she determined the call was work related.

The deep tones of Drake's voice carried over to Cleo but she couldn't make out the words. He glanced towards her and smiled before making several notes at his desk. She watched him as he replaced the telephone receiver and walked back towards her. He moved with the grace of a cat and she was reminded of Mariana's comment. She smiled.

"I'm sorry, Cleo, but I'm needed in the studio. I'll walk you down."

As she stood up and followed him out of his office she realized she would've liked having dinner with the man in front of her. His invitation must have been impulsive because he hadn't brought the subject up since he returned from taking the phone call.

"Rita, will you validate Ms. Martin's parking ticket for her?" Drake asked the older woman politely. She produced the ticket and watched as the assistant stamped it. Another short minute ticked by as they stood by the doors of the elevator, waiting for it to arrive.

Her mind raced as she stood next to him. She could smell the spicy scent of his aftershave and she wondered if he'd ask her to dinner again. The warning signal she'd gotten earlier about Drake being trouble was both frightening and alluring. Cleo wondered what it would be like to be involved with a man like Drake Stockton.

Cleo was surprised when the doors of the elevator opened on the twenty-seventh floor and Drake extended his arm indicating she should exit the car.

"Come to the studio with me for a minute," and Drake led her down the same corridor she'd entered when she had auditioned.

Drake pushed open the studio door and they walked inside. The three men from behind the glass partition were now sitting in several of the theater-style seats. Cleo saw Mariana was with them, along with several other production people.

The group was talking softly and the sound of laughter lifted into the air, along with smoke from someone's cigarette. It was getting late in the afternoon and the people in the room were relaxing after a long day's work.

When Drake and Cleo walked towards the group, one of the older men saw them and announced their arrival. The group snapped to attention and started to applaud and cheer. Drake certainly seemed to command the respect of people who worked at TSA.

"Well, Charlie, do you want to make the announcement or shall I?" Drake asked as the applause began to subside.

"Oh, I think you should, Drake, after all it's your company," Charlie responded.

"But it's your project..." Drake bantered with Charlie. Cleo felt a knot form in her stomach as she watched the two men. She tried to tell herself their exchange had nothing to do with her. She was just a bystander, included by chance.

Charlie and Drake decided to make a joint announcement and they turned to address the group.

"Everyone," Drake started. "It's our pleasure to introduce you to the new 'Healthy Shine' shampoo girl —"

"Cleo Martin!" Charlie finished. The applause started again and Cleo felt faint. The near impossible had happened. The dream she was afraid to dream but tried to find every day was hers — she had an acting job! She had a national commercial! It was great and it felt wonderful. The knot in her stomach unwound into excited energy.

The group of people in the room gathered around her and offered their congratulations while Cleo tried to assimilate the news. What did she do now? Of course, she'd have to call Raymond and let him know. She'd have to sign a contract and work out the shooting schedule but she knew everything would fall into place over the next couple of days.

Cleo saw Drake standing away from the crowd. She caught his eye and he smiled. As she returned his smile she wondered how much influence he'd had on the decision making process.

A feeling of dread rose inside her, quelling the excitement she'd felt moments before. Drake Stockton wasn't going to pull strings for her, especially if he thought he was making up for the evening before. Maybe she was jumping to conclusions, but she didn't want the job if she hadn't earned it fair and square.

Cleo excused herself from the group around her and walked over to Drake. She wasn't sure how to ask him and she struggled to find the right words.

"What type of input did you have on the decision to hire me?" There. She'd asked him.

"To be honest, none," Drake replied slowly. She had trouble believing him.

"I have a creative team working on this account. It's their project. The people you have to thank are standing right over there," Drake continued, gesturing towards the group. "I haven't even seen your screen test."

Cleo let out the breath she'd been holding. "Good. I wouldn't want to get off on the wrong foot."

"Which foot would that be?"

"The left one, of course, not the right," Cleo was quick to answer. Drake liked her quick wit although it concerned him she thought he pulled strings to get her the commercial.

"I really don't know you well enough to jeopardize my company for you, do I, Cleo?" Drake felt a pain inside as the image of another blonde woman flashed in his mind. He'd made that mistake one time already. It was a mistake he wouldn't allow to happen again.

She felt her cheeks warm as she realized she'd exaggerated his feelings of obligation for Randy's behavior the evening before.

"And besides," Drake continued, "I certainly don't feel obligated to correct another man's blunder, regardless of who he is."

"I'm sorry, it's just that I want to be selected based on my own merit, nothing more." I guess we won't be having dinner after all, Cleo thought as she re-joined the group.

"Well, that's a wrap for today, folks." Charlie addressed the production staff around him. "We're going to start shooting Wednesday, so you know what that means... get lots of sleep tonight and get yourselves geared up for pre-production!" Several people let out exaggerated groans that turned into laughter as Charlie started to shoo people towards the door, including Cleo.

"Glad to have you on board. We'll get the standard contract over to Raymond on Monday." Charlie shook Cleo's hand before she stepped aboard the elevator. "And we'll see you bright and early Wednesday!"

As the elevator doors closed quietness engulfed her. Somehow the recent events seemed to blur together and only when the elevator doors opened at the marble lobby of the building did she realize the full implications of getting a commercial. She had a job, an income, doing exactly what she wanted to do — act!

I wonder how much TSA pays someone to be in one of their commercials, Cleo pondered as she pushed open the glass doors leading to the street outside. *Who cares, I've got a job!* She felt like laughing out loud. Just yesterday she was convinced an acting job far out of reach. What a difference one day could make.

Raymond! She had to call him and tell him the good news. And her parents! And Ju-Dee! There were so many people she wanted to let know. She let herself into her apartment and picked up the receiver of her phone. After four rings, Raymond's machine picked up and she left him a teasing, cryptic message.

"That should make him curious." Cleo laughed.

Next she dialed her parents. Again, the only

answer she got was their machine. "Hi, it's Cleo. I've got some great news. Call me when you get in." It felt a little hollow, leaving a message on an answering machine.

After several more calls and brief messages on answering machines, she hadn't connected with anyone in person.

Cleo loved her parents and she felt her wonderful group of friends made up an extended family, but it was times like this she felt a little self-pity. Here she sat, alone in her apartment with great news and she had no one to share the good news with. Being twenty-seven without a man in her life could be downright lonely. And yet it was by choice. She refused to derail herself from her goal of acting. She could not afford to be distracted by a man. She'd seen too many women sacrifice their own dreams for another person and it scared her that she could lose herself in a relationship.

Regardless, whenever she decided to date more seriously, she wanted to find a man who complimented her mentally, emotionally and physically. She wanted a man who could be her best friend and her lover. It seemed the men in her past had been able to be one or the other but not both.

Cleo looked at her watch and let out a sigh. She had to be at Podium soon. At least she could share her big news with Ju-Dee and Rock. Not quite the same as having a boyfriend to share her news with but both were good friends. She felt fidgety and she wandered around her small apartment. Unable to sit still, she finally grabbed her keys and black satchel and headed for the door. At least she'd be able to see her extended family at Podium and dance away her excessive energy.

The phone began to ring as she reached her front door. She felt excited as she reached for it. Hopefully it was her parents returning her call. She could hardly wait to share her news — they'd been supportive but skeptical about her following in her grandmother's footsteps.

She couldn't have been further from the truth. The voice on the other end of the line was becoming all too familiar. She hung up the phone without saying a word, shutting out the lurid comments from the other end.

CHAPTER THREE

"I have speed!"

In the background a loud bell rang reminding Cleo of a high school fire drill. Commotion on the set quieted and the Loader announced the scene and clapped the smart slate together. The director yelled, "Action!"

She performed the scene, as rehearsed, without a hitch.

"Cut!" The director looked at her and said "That was great, honey," before he consulted with the production crew around him.

She'd been on the set for the entire morning and the surroundings amazed her. They'd shot several scenes already and were in the process of setting up the next one. New terminology such as "speed," which indicated rolling film, was foreign to her.

I wonder if the novelty of being on a set ever fades, Cleo thought. *Does anyone ever take this in stride, seeing this as a normal, ordinary job?* She hoped not. She loved every minute. Even the hurry up and wait aspects.

Cleo learned there were times when the production crew needed to construct a set, change lighting and check props. All consumed time and she wandered around and watched.

As she strolled around the set watching the activity around her, she fought the urge to run her fingers through her hair. Considering this commercial was being shot to convince television viewers Healthy Shine shampoo made life easier, she'd undergone a tedious and time consuming makeover leaving her hair layered with mousse, gel and hairspray. Running her fingers through her hair would only subject her to more torturous maneuvers by the hair stylist.

An abundance of food was on location. Everything from gooey pastries to vegetable platters, all designed to meet a variety of appetites. She wandered over to a table laden with food and picked up several carrot sticks.

She'd been watching for Drake but he was nowhere to be seen. She'd had mixed emotions the evening before, worrying he might be on the set. She was afraid he might show and yet, secretly, more frightened that he might not.

Just when Cleo finished convincing herself Drake was too busy to attend the filming of a simple commercial, she saw him sitting in a chair next to the director. How long had he been there? Certainly not long or she would've noticed him sooner. She felt nervous energy flare at the sight of him and had trouble finishing the carrot stick she was nibbling on.

The thought of Drake not coming to the set had disappointed her but she didn't want to examine her feelings more closely. She also didn't want to think about the leap of joy that surged inside her at the sight of him sitting so gracefully next to the director. She remembered Mariana's comment about him being akin to a cat and she had to agree, although definitely not a housecat. He looked so perfect, like he belonged there. She'd been feeling a little out of place on the set. Now that several scenes were completed she was beginning to feel more comfortable.

With all the auditions she'd been on, she felt at home in front of a camera. However, she wasn't aware of all the protocols that went along with working as an actress. Her one other paid acting job working on the low budget film, *Bingo Baby*, had been a no-frills job.

Nothing had prepared her for today. Nothing had prepared her for the pampering of a makeup artist and hairstylist. Nothing had prepared her for the assistants that were ready to carry out even her simplest wish. No wonder actors or actresses could develop an attitude after getting all this attention. She felt more comfortable without the hoopla.

"Cleo, honey, come on over here. I want to introduce you to Drake Stockton," the director called across the room. As she approached he continued, "Drake's the owner of The Stockton Agency, the advertising firm that's producing this commercial."

"Actually, James, we've already met – on the day she auditioned. Hello, Cleo." There was that wonderful voice again. And so formal. Everyone else on the set called the director Jamie.

Cleo hadn't spoken to Drake since Saturday. There were so many things she wanted to say and all that came out was "Hi, Drake." She was surprised she didn't see a butterfly emerge as she opened her mouth to speak, considering how many she felt fluttering around inside.

"James told me this morning went very well."

"Yes." *Well, I guess I'm mastering the art of single syllable conversation,* Cleo thought wryly. "It's been a lot of fun." *Not much better but at least I've graduated to sentences with a noun and verb*, she scolded herself as she tried to think of something to say.

Luckily Drake took control of the conversation and she just had to listen to the two men in front of her as they spoke about the commercial. She began to feel like an eavesdropper and she wondered if they needed her there or whether she should excuse herself.

Before she'd had the chance to decide, Drake turned towards her. "It's going to be an hour before this set is completed. How about getting something to eat?" There was that tone again. It was phrased as a question but the authority was there, making her wonder if she really had a choice. It didn't matter, she was sure lunch with Drake Stockton would be an interesting experience.

She looked towards Jamie. He seemed to sense her unasked question and grinned. "Have fun, Cleo. I'm not about to argue with the man who signs my paychecks. If he wants to take the talent out for lunch, I'll just step aside."

"Then it's settled. Let's go." Drake moved quickly and Cleo was several steps behind him, trying to keep up.

She groaned internally, wondering how she was going to be able to eat a meal with him. Between the butterflies swarming inside her stomach and all the food she'd eaten during the lapses in filming, a large meal was the last thing she wanted. But the desire to learn more about the man she followed compelled her forward.

She marveled again at how different Drake Stockton was from other men she knew. Just watching his strong, broad shoulders and his back which angled down to a trim waist and firm...

She mentally shook herself. Drake Stockton

brought out a side of her she didn't know existed.
He awakened something deep inside her. She felt
like a magnet was pulling her forward and she
didn't want to fight it.

❧

Drake quickly unlocked his 500SL Mercedes
and opened the door for Cleo. *What am I doing
here?*, he chastised himself. I've been down this
road once before and it was one time too many. He
tried to push thoughts of Gabriella out of his mind.
One blonde actress had been enough.

Drake promised himself he would take Cleo to
lunch, nothing more. He'd been surprised how fre-
quently she slipped into his thoughts since the
night at Podium and after meeting her again at his
office.

It had been awhile since someone sparked his
curiosity the way Cleo had the afternoon of the auditions. During lunch he was sure that he would
find Cleo was like every other actress in Los Angeles — self-motivated, selfish and self-centered.
Gabriella had shown him that.

Lunch. That ought to do it. It wouldn't take too
much longer to find out about this woman. Most
actresses in Los Angeles would tell their life's story
over lunch especially if they thought it would get
them a part.

Cleo slid into the leather seat of Drake's car
and looked over at him as he settled behind the
wheel and started the engine. He looked different
today. He was dressed similarly to the previous
times she'd seen him but he had a determined look
on his face. Cleo wondered what he was thinking.

The expression on Drake's face changed as he
turned towards her. "Are you a vegetarian? Macro-

biotic? Fasting?"

Cleo had to laugh. "No, nope, and definitely not!"

"So you'll eat meat?" he asked as he drove off the studio lot.

"What exactly do you have in mind?"

"Believe it or not, I've been craving a chili-dog and fries from Carney's."

"You're kidding!" Cleo looked over at Drake Stockton. Dressed in an expensive Italian suit, driving an expensive German car and he wanted to get the all-American meal.

"Let's go. I wouldn't mind having a Chicago dog."

"Ah, a woman who's familiar with the Carney's menu. I like that," Drake laughed as he accelerated his car down Barham Boulevard, heading towards Sunset. Drake's laugh was rich and deep and it reminded Cleo how she'd first thought he never laughed or smiled. She was glad she'd been wrong.

Carney's was nestled along Sunset Strip near the St. James Club. Carney's was a landmark of its own, housed in a bright yellow train car. Black and white photos hung along the serving line, showing the procession of the railroad car on Sunset Boulevard as it was delivered to its current location decades earlier.

Drake confirmed what Cleo wanted and ordered for both of them. They watched as several people behind the counter quickly prepared each order, placing the food into cardboard boxes on the counter. Within minutes they were walking towards a table, carrying boxes full of food and drinks. "Do you want to sit inside or out on the patio?"

"Inside," Cleo responded quickly and they

pulled out chairs at a table with a view of Sunset Boulevard. "I have fair skin and without sun protection, I'll fry outside," Cleo explained after they were seated.

Drake watched Cleo take a bite out of her hot dog, loaded with the works, and then take a sip of her drink. Eating a Carney's Chicago style chili-dog required finesse, gusto and lots of napkins. Drake thought she looked right at home as she poured ketchup into her cardboard box and started generously dipping her French fries and popping them into her mouth, one by one.

She was glad Drake wanted to come here. She never had any trouble eating food from Carney's. She felt at home here and the butterflies she'd felt earlier were gone.

Drake settled in and finally took his eyes off Cleo long enough to take a bite out of his own hotdog. It tasted good and he was glad he'd thought to bring her here. Just watching her eat was an experience. She definitely threw herself into everything she did. She ate the same way she danced — with carefree abandon.

"So tell me about yourself," Drake encouraged Cleo between bites of his meal. That type of request would have kept Gabriella talking for hours.

"Well, there's not much to tell. What about you? How'd you get started in advertising?" Cleo volleyed the conversational ball back into his court.

"Long story. What caused you to pursue acting?" He intercepted and shot the conversation back towards her. *That question should get her talking*, Drake thought.

"Well, that's hard to explain, especially with chili running down my arm," Cleo laughed, avoiding his question while reaching for a napkin. She didn't like to talk about herself and found it much more interesting finding out what motivated other people. That curiosity was one of the reasons she'd pursued acting. She liked deciphering people and using the various things she discovered to assume different roles and convey a variety of characters.

The conversation continued back and forth between them with both trying to get the other to start talking about themselves first. Frustrated, Drake finally leaned back in his chair and started to laugh. "You don't like talking about yourself, do you Cleo?"

"Apparently about as much as you do," Cleo laughed in response.

"Touché. Okay, truce." Drake surrendered and then he was struck with an idea. "Have you ever played the game Twenty Questions?"

Cleo hesitated, drawing out her reply. "Ye..es."

"Okay, let's try it. We both get to ask each other twenty questions but they have to be short answer types of things. No religion, politics or the meaning of life stuff. Are you game?"

"Animal, vegetable or mineral?" Cleo asked playfully.

"Animal, although after a long day at the office I sometimes feel like a vegetable. You have nineteen questions left."

"Oh! you're serious!" Cleo laughed. Here she was with Drake Stockton, eating stick-to-the-ribs kind of food and playing an impromptu game of Twenty Questions.

"Okay, it's my turn. What's your favorite color?" Drake asked, starting with something neutral.

"Green. No wait, purple. Maybe red. I don't know. I don't like brown, too drab. What's yours?"

Drake thought for a minute. It'd been a long time since anyone had asked him to pick his favorite color. He felt like he was back in high school. He'd been feeling that way a lot since he'd met her. He looked into Cleo's blue eyes and tried to think of an answer. It was staring him right in the face. "Blue," he answered quietly.

"What's your favorite food?"

"Besides Carney's?" Drake clarified. "Chinese."

Cleo laughed. This was fun and it felt safe. "What do you order?"

"Anything spicy. What about you?"

Cleo thought for a few seconds. "Egg rolls and wonton soup."

"Take-out or dine in?"

"Take-out, definitely." Cleo wondered what it would be like to order take-out with Drake, opening little cartons and eating with chopsticks. "Have you ever been to China?"

"No, although I've been to Japan," Drake answered. "What about you?"

"I've only traveled in the United States except for a day trip to Mexico with some friends a couple months ago."

"Where would you go if you could go anywhere?"

Cleo had a wistful expression on her face when she answered. "Italy. I'd really like to go to Venice."

Italy. And Venice, one of the most romantic cities in the world with all those canals and gondolas. Drake speculated what it would be like to explore Venice with the spunky, blonde woman who sat across from him.

Beep. Beep. Beep. The incessant sound interrupted their game and Cleo watched as Drake pulled out a pager and pressed a button, stopping the noise.

"That's Rita reminding me of my next appointment." Drake looked at his watch and let out a sigh. "I'm sorry, Cleo, but I've got to cut our game short. James is expecting you back on set and I've got a meeting I have to attend."

Lunch certainly hadn't been what he'd expected. He'd hoped to appease his curiosity then get back to work. For the last several years, work had been his life. No one, at least no one until Cleo, had distracted him for any length of time. Not since he'd thrown Gabriella out of his apartment two years ago.

If anything, this tantalizing game of cat and mouse, or Twenty Questions, he was playing with Cleo was only whetting his appetite. He was beginning to realize what had been missing in his life during the past couple of years.

Most of the people around Drake tried to tell him what they thought he wanted to hear. At the audition she'd been refreshingly different. But how much of this was an act? She was obviously masterful at manipulating a conversation or at least avoiding deep personal revelations.

❧

Cleo was surprised. Her previous encounters with Drake had been relatively formal and this casual bantering lunch over chili-dogs and sodas was certainly a switch.

At other industry lunches, Cleo found herself being probed for information she didn't want to share. She'd become sensitive about revealing only what she wanted and steering the conversation away from her whenever it was necessary.

Drake seemed to be different but Cleo was still

wary. It was obvious to her that he was trying to find out something about her and she wondered why. *Did he really want to get to know her, the person, or was he just interested in filling time?*

Too many times before she'd been aware of men trying to find out her dreams and aspirations to manipulate her. Cleo thought it was disgusting some men would suggest physical interludes with the promise of a part in a movie or other production project. A part she knew would never materialize.

She already had the commercial and there had been no hint at a physical payback for getting the part. But there was something she couldn't quite put her finger on. Something made her question his motives. Cleo was an expert when it came to understanding people and there was something Drake Stockton wasn't sharing.

Drake guided Cleo out to his car and helped her inside before walking around to climb in behind the steering wheel. He turned the key in the ignition and the car roared to life.

Cleo marveled at the man who sat next to her. He certainly was multi-faceted. The laughing, playful man from lunch was gone. The laugh lines that crinkled during their meal were smooth now as he propelled his car into traffic. The formal, business Drake had returned and it was hard to imagine him any other way. If she hadn't witnessed the glimpse of the inner Drake Stockton during lunch she would've sworn that side of him didn't exist. It was a side of him she hoped to see again.

The drive back to the studio lot was short and they hardly spoke. It was a comfortable silence and she was thankful she had the time to reflect on their lunch before getting back to the commercial.

"Are you filming the beach shots tomorrow?" Drake's question interrupted her thoughts.

"Yes! I'm not sure how all these scenes fit together yet but it's been a lot of fun." So far they'd shot a variety of indoor settings at the studio. The following day was going to be devoted to filming a group of outdoor activities. Everything from playing Frisbee on the beach with a golden retriever to a family barbecue. She'd no idea they would've been able to fit so many things into three days of filming.

"I'll make sure you get an advance copy of the commercial so you can see the end result. Trust me, it'll make sense when you see the finished product," Drake assured her as they pulled into the studio parking lot.

"Oh, I'm not worried," Cleo laughed. "Just curious." She unlatched her seat belt and opened the car door. "Are you going to be on location tomorrow?"

"Unfortunately, no. I'm flying up to San Francisco for a business meeting that's going to take up the majority of my day."

"Oh." Cleo didn't know what to say. She felt a twinge of homesickness at the mention of her hometown. It'd been awhile since she'd been able to visit her family and friends up north. She extended her hand toward Drake, "Thank you for lunch, I had a nice time."

"Me too," he replied sincerely as he grasped her hand briefly.

"Have a good meeting tomorrow," Cleo said as she shut her car door.

"Have fun on location," Drake put his car in reverse. "Sorry to eat and run but work beckons."

"Yeah, for both of us," Cleo waved goodbye before turning towards the large warehouse which contained the sound studio. She didn't know why, but she felt sad watching Drake drive away.

"Oh good, Cleo, you're back," Mariana called over to her as she walked inside. 'Raymond called while you were gone and he sounded totally panic-stricken. He made me promise to drag you to a phone when you got back from lunch. Have no fear, I dragged the phone to you." Mariana reached into the pocket of her jacket and pulled out a portable cellular phone.

Cleo felt a wave of panic wash over her. It seemed unlikely that Raymond would call her on location. She looked at Mariana. "What about the filming? Do I have time to call?"

"Don't worry, we aren't going to start shooting again for at least ten minutes," the young woman reassured her. "Why don't you use the trailer out back and I'll come get you when we're ready."

Cleo was thankful for the other woman's support. With all the commotion on the set she welcomed the privacy of the trailer. Her fingers shook as she dialed Raymond's number and she hoped everything was alright.

CHAPTER FOUR

"That's a wrap, everybody. See you tomorrow, bright and early," the director called out to the crew. "Cleo, get a good night's sleep tonight because tomorrow is going to be a long day. Mariana will give you details."

Cleo was thankful she'd taken the next several nights off from the club. It was almost eight in the evening and all Cleo wanted was a bath and to tuck herself into her cozy bed. The previous night she'd been too excited to sleep and the day had been long. Her body was finally giving way to its exhaustion.

Mariana filled Cleo in on the next day's events as they walked to the parking lot. "We're shooting at Santa Monica pier first thing tomorrow and then we'll be moving onto the sandy part of the beach. The sun can really zap your energy. You might want to bring a large hat with you if you have one. Between the wind and the salt we're already going to be re-doing your hair a lot so I don't think a hat is going to make much difference."

Cleo thanked Mariana for all her assistance. The day had been strenuous and Mariana had been delightful. Cleo wondered if they would remain friends after the commercial shoot was over. She had learned in her few years in Los Angeles that often times people were friendly but didn't make an effort after getting what they needed for the work they were doing. It hadn't taken long to construct her armor and to protect herself. Los Angeles could be a cruel town whose inhabitants judged people on how they looked and not by who they were inside.

"Where are you parked?" Mariana asked as they approached the few cars that were still in the parking lot.

"This is mine," Cleo gestured towards her motorcycle.

"I LOVE it! Do you really ride that?" Mariana asked excitedly. "Promise me you'll take me for a ride sometime."

Although she was tired, Cleo laughed. "Sure, maybe tomorrow between shots." Mariana was like a kid in a candy shop and her energy was contagious. She wasn't showing any signs of slowing down even after a long day on the commercial set.

The cool evening air washed over Cleo as she manipulated her bike through the back roads, avoiding the Los Angeles freeway system. She finally had time to reflect on her call with Raymond. Everything was a drama to her agent. She'd been so worried when she sat down in the trailer to call him. Raymond was every bit a professional and Cleo knew it would have to be something important for him to interrupt her while she was on a job.

Cleo had tried to think of the various reasons Raymond would have called as she dialed his number. It couldn't be the contract for the Healthy Shine commercials. The documents had been sent over earlier in the week and everything was signed, sealed and delivered before shooting began so Cleo dismissed that from her mind. What else could it be?

It didn't take long for Raymond's assistant to answer the phone and transfer Cleo's call. She let out a sigh of relief when Raymond assured her that everything was alright.

"Cleo, are you sitting down?"

"Yes," Cleo lied as she paced the small trailer.

"Remember I told you Bill Meyerson's casting his next film? Well, Cathy Rodriguez is doing the preliminary casting and she wants to have you read next Monday!" Raymond spoke hurriedly and excitedly on the other end of the phone, stringing his words together.

Cleo felt her legs go weak and she gripped the back of a chair for support. Cathy Rodriguez was well known and worked for a high caliber casting company. This was the opportunity of a lifetime. Cleo tried to focus on what Raymond was saying.

"Cathy's office is going to send over the sides by Friday so you'll have all weekend to look them over. Honey, I'm soooo excited!" Raymond was practically cooing into the phone.

Cleo started to giggle listening to Raymond. When it rains it truly did pour. She didn't know what she'd done lately but apparently it was something right. First she landed the commercial and now the Bill Meyerson audition.

Cleo didn't want to get her hopes up too high. This was only the first casting call of potentially many that could lead to a part in the Bill Meyerson production. Chances were there would be at least three readings to land a role of this magnitude and that was only if she made each cut. Cleo's reading on Monday would be the first step. A step lots of other actresses were bound to be taking as well.

Bill Meyerson was definitely big time. Raymond must have pulled a lot of strings to get her the reading. Her acting experience included some theater, television bit-parts and several student films, but overall her professional feature film credits were slim with only one spoken line in a low budget film that had gone directly to video stores.

Thinking about the Bill Meyerson audition caused Cleo's nervous energy to return. She knew she was physically exhausted but her mind was racing a mile a minute. The role she would be auditioning for on Monday sounded exciting and definitely unique. Even Raymond had trouble explaining the intricacies of the part. Cleo could hardly wait to get the sides to examine.

Cleo pulled her motorcycle into her driveway, thankful she would finally be able to wash the layers of sprays and gels from her hair. The first day of shooting was over. One third of the job had been completed and Cleo was saddened to think that there were only two more days left. What an exhilarating day! She tried not to think too much about her encounter with Drake Stockton. From the sound of things she would probably never see him again anyway. His hectic schedule would have him shuttling off to a variety of meetings and the shoot would be over soon.

Drake had promised her an advance copy of the commercial but Cleo highly doubted he would be involved with the administrative efforts to deliver the tape. The production staff, probably Mariana, would be responsible for getting her a copy. Luckily for Cleo, the post-production time for a commercial varied from feature films. It could be just a few short weeks, or even days, before the commercial received air time. Post-production time for a feature film could be months, or in some cases, a year or more.

She thought back to the one-liner she had in the film, *Bingo Baby*. It had gone directly to the video stores without ever having a theater release. She smiled as she remembered that the film had sat on a shelf for months collecting dust, while the studio tried to figure out how to promote it.

Originally her part had more than one line and she had actually been part of the filming for a week. She smiled as she remembered the video screening she had had with several friends when the film had finally been released. One line. That was all that had remained of her work. Her friends had laughed and tried to appease her with bingo humor. "I guess that was "B-4" editing."

Just because you worked on a project didn't necessarily mean that you were in the project. Even Kevin Costner had been completely cut out of *The Big Chill*, except for the shot of him in a coffin at the beginning of the film.

Drake Stockton. His name flashed into her mind quickly and she wondered why she had transitioned from a reflection on her career to the professional man. Cleo was sure he'd never had to struggle with success. From the look of TSA he'd done quite well. Cleo was sure Drake Stockton never had to worry about his place in his work. They were from different worlds that just happened to overlap and Cleo felt the magnet pulling her towards him again.

She'd wanted to continue their game of Twenty Questions and ask him a variety of things. Some were safe, simple questions that would give her more insight into his character. Others would allow her to understand the man he was both in and out of the office. Questions had run through her mind throughout lunch and into the afternoon. Questions that she was sure were off limits by definition of the game. They delved from basic to the more philosophical side of Drake Stockton. Was he a morning person? How did he like to spend his evenings? Who did he vote for? How did he feel about family?

Family. What would Drake be like, surrounded by children? Cleo didn't know why but she was sure he'd be a great father.

Cleo wondered if he really worked all the time. After all, he'd been working the night he showed up at Podium with Randy. Cleo had a hard time imagining Drake Stockton in anything but an expensive business suit but she knew he'd look good in anything he wore. She tried to strip him of his corporate attire, wrapping him in a variety of clothing, testing out different styles on the imaginary Drake doll in her mind.

Cleo was convinced that he'd look amazing in faded jeans, if he even owned a pair. Jeans, with a white cotton shirt with all its buttons loose, untucked, revealing his bare chest. No shoes, no socks and a mug of coffee and Cleo was sure that she had an accurate picture of Drake Stockton on a Sunday morning, preparing to scour through the daily paper. Add rumpled hair and a little morning stubble and in Cleo's mind he looked almost downright boyish. Almost.

She really did have an overactive imagination and too much nervous energy as she realized where her thoughts had taken her. She tossed and turned in bed, trying to fluff and mash the pillows into a more comfortable position as she tried to push the thoughts of Drake Stockton out of her mind. It was highly unlikely that she would ever see him again. Cleo felt a twinge of regret and sadness at the thought that she would be deprived of the opportunity to get to know him better and yet she knew it was for the best. She'd been working a long time to make it as an actress and she needed to stay focused. Besides, Drake owned the advertising agency and she knew better than to mix business with pleasure.

❧

It was two in the morning and Drake Stockton was having trouble sleeping. What annoyed him the most was that he never had trouble sleeping. Never. He balled his hand into a fist and pounded the pillow for the umpteenth time and collapsed, ordering his body to shut down and sleep for the rest of the night.

His mind had different ideas and replayed the events of his lunch with Cleo Martin. There were so many questions he'd wanted to ask her. The more she clammed up the more he wanted to know. Drake was sure that Freud would have an idea or two about that.

His idea to play twenty questions had successfully broken down Cleo's reserves. Well, somewhat anyway, and Drake was disappointed the game had ended so soon. Damn work, damn meetings.

Ever since he'd run into Cleo at the audition he'd been having trouble putting her out of his mind. And he was having a harder time keeping the thought of work top of mind. Maybe he needed a vacation. He hadn't truly had one in the past three years. A weekend or two here and there but certainly not a bonafide vacation away from the phone and fax.

"Damn it!" Drake muttered as he sat upright in bed. This certainly isn't doing me any good, he thought as he threw back the covers and stood up. It would be better to get something accomplished rather than toss and turn all night.

Drake pulled a pair of faded jeans over the pair of silk, paisley boxer shorts he was wearing. The cool night air wrapped around his smooth skin and he decided to pull on a shirt as well. He grabbed the white cotton shirt he had removed earlier and carelessly thrown on the chair by his bed. He didn't bother to button it as he walked, barefoot, down the carpeted hallway to his home office.

He raked his hands through his hair as he sat down at his desk. He placed his briefcase onto the desktop in front of him and pulled out a variety of papers and settled down to work.

The next two days of the commercial shoot were exhilarating and flew by quickly. Cleo felt a mixture of emotions when the director called "Cut!" for the last time, knowing it could be awhile before she worked again as a paid actress. Her auditions would continue but an actual paying part could be a long way away.

Ju-Dee had dropped by to observe some of the filming on the last day and she had also wondered how all the pieces of footage were going to fit together into a commercial. Cleo had been filmed on the beach running with a golden retriever, riding the merry-go-round at Santa Monica pier with a young blonde child, working at a corporate office and numerous other situations. As far as Cleo and Ju-Dee could tell, none of it tied together.

"You're going to have to let me know when this commercial is going to be on," Ju-Dee solicited her

Friend.

"Mariana told me it's going to have national rotation. It'll be airing in a variety of time slots, during everything from the evening news to *Oprah*." The full implications of what that meant had not really sunk in. Apparently Cleo's face was going to be seen as much as if it adorned the front of a Wheaties box. And, since she was the principle in the commercial, she knew she would not end up on the cutting room floor along with the remains of *Bingo Baby*.

❧

Monday arrived and the first audition for the Bill Meyerson production went well. Since it would be the first of many potential casting calls, her nerves were at a minimum. She knew if she were to get a call back her nerves would be stretched a little tighter when she went for the second reading. Tighter still, if there was a third.

The sides that Raymond had dropped off at her apartment hinted at a wonderful script and left Cleo wanting more. The character, a Nancy Drew type that went looking for trouble rather than solutions, was a comic, mystical blend. Besides having the practicality of the young detective, she possessed an element of erotism and, from the few pages of the script that Cleo possessed, it appeared she had half the men in her small hometown chasing after her, trying to get her into bed.

Cleo was enchanted by the character. It would be fun to play a role that had men worshipping you, Cleo thought playfully. Cleo knew she didn't have that problem in her real life. She hadn't heard a word from Drake Stockton since their lunch at

Carneys and she was sure he had put her completely out of his mind.

She'd called Ju-Dee's friend, Larry, after he had left a message on her answering machine but their meeting for coffee had left Cleo discouraged. Her encounter with Larry made Cleo wonder what Ju-Dee had been thinking when she had thought that Cleo and Larry would make a good match. Cleo had tried not to measure Larry against Drake Stockton, feeling it was unfair to make comparisons, especially when Larry failed so miserably in the process. Why was she obsessing over the corporate executive after one lunch? Besides, she wasn't even looking for anything of substance right now. She had to focus on her career. A man would only be a distraction from her goals.

One thing was for sure, she was done with blind dates. So much for having men falling at your feet. Cleo was sure that could only happen in the movies. Cleo felt a wave of fear wash over her as she realized the casting company might be looking for a woman all men lusted for, blindly throwing themselves at her feet. Maybe there was such a woman in the real world, not only the reel world.

The fear that had gripped her momentarily made Cleo aware of how important it was to her to get the part in the Bill Meyerson film. Normally she wasn't so emotionally involved. That type of involvement could kill you, considering the level of rejection there was with acting.

This script was different. It was good and challenging. Cleo could smell it. Cleo wanted it. The impact of that realization sent another type of fear rippling through her that was more frightening than the first.

Cleo took several deep breaths and tried to calm her racing heart. This strong desire to get the Meyerson film caused a wave of anxiety that left Cleo's pulse racing. It was strange to be caught up in emotional turmoil and Cleo felt it contradicted her view of herself. She'd have to find a way to emotionally distance herself from the role. She'd have to hope for the best but be prepared for the worst.

After coming to that personal resolution, it was easier to examine the root of the strong desire she felt inside. Cleo decided the Bill Meyerson role symbolized everything she felt would enable her to act as much as she wanted, in the capacity she wanted. Knowing this made it easier to face her fears and control her strong desire for the part. She wanted success for herself but also for her grandmother who had always encouraged her to pursue her dreams. Cleo absentmindedly twirled the gold bracelet on her wrist between her thumb and forefinger.

Raymond had told her it could be several weeks before they got back to her regarding a second reading. Better to keep her fingers crossed and put the thoughts of the audition out of her mind.

When casting a film it was not uncommon for the casting company to keep looking, even after finding someone they thought fit the role, just to feel confident in their decision. With the amount of money involved in making a film, it was important to be comfortable about the final casting especially if the actress selected didn't have a name familiar to the viewing public. She tried not to think about all the actresses that the public already knew who would also be interested in being part of a Meyerson film. All the more reason not to get her hopes up.

❧

Several weeks went by and Cleo settled into her familiar routine. Auditions by day and dancing at Podium by night. Luckily the disturbing calls from the mysterious man had subsided. She'd only received one during the past few weeks. He must have grown tired of pursuing her, realizing it was pointless.

She'd reluctantly pushed the thoughts of Drake Stockton out of her mind. She'd thought about calling him but felt uncomfortable when she reached for the phone. Better to leave well enough alone.

At first she'd been hopeful he might contact her when he returned from San Francisco but with each passing day her hope faded. Hope was like the flickering flame of a candle. The flame was forced to extinguish itself when it reached the end of the wick.

She'd reached the end of her wick and that was one reason she had to blink twice when she entered Podium to make sure she wasn't looking at a hallucination.

The club hadn't opened yet and Cleo wished there were people surrounding her, making it possible for her to drift into a crowd, unnoticed. She wasn't ready for this impending encounter with Drake Stockton. She'd just gotten used to the idea of never seeing him again. How dare he waltz in now?

Cleo tried not to giggle out loud. She thought she sounded like a jilted lover and she'd only gone out to lunch with him once. What kind of power did this man have over her? Why did she feel so possessive of Drake Stockton? He hadn't offered her anything. He hadn't even promised her anything. She didn't know if she should laugh or scream at the absurdity of the situation.

"Hello, Cleo." Yup, there was that smooth voice. Already it seemed so familiar to her.

"Hi, Drake. Long time, no see." She tried to sound casual. Churn, churn. Her body was starting to crank out the butterflies. "So what brings you to Podium? I don't see Randy in tow." The memory of the first night he'd come to the club was clearer than she would have liked.

Instead of wearing a suit like he had the first night she'd seen him, he was dressed more casually in a sweater, khakis, loafers and a black leather jacket. Maybe he was here on a social visit.

"Randy has returned to New York. His business in Los Angeles is finished. For now." Cleo was hoping that Drake would look flustered, uncomfortable. She wanted him to mirror how she felt but she wasn't that lucky. He looked like he fit right in, cool and smooth.

"Actually, I wanted to bring you an advance copy of the commercial. It's going to start airing Monday. I've also included a rotation schedule if you're interested in watching it live instead of on tape."

"Oh." Apparently Cleo was right when she'd thought he never did anything but work. She didn't know why she thought this would be a social visit. "Thanks for bringing me a copy." Cleo reached out and took the video cassette case Drake extended towards her.

"Well, I promised to drop it by."

"Yeah. Thanks again."

"Hey, Cleo, honey. Let me know if that guy's bothering you." Rock's voice boomed across the dance floor. "He told me he worked for that commercial company but I'll eighty-six 'em if I need to." Rock's eyes glinted good-naturedly as he approached.

Cleo had to laugh as the large bouncer gave her a quick hug. "I see you've met my bodyguard," she said.

"Drake Stockton." Drake extended his hand to Rock.

"Henry Wilson." Rock grasped Drake's hand firmly and didn't let go. In his lower, more menacing bouncer voice he continued. "But people call me 'Rock'." He let go of Drake's hand and laughed, the intimidating presence evaporating into thin air. "Can I get you a drink?" He looked questioningly towards Drake and then Cleo. When neither of them answered immediately, Rock continued. "Ancient custom. People sitting around a campfire, sharing stories over a meal. I can't offer you a fire or a meal but I can promise you a good story over a drink." Rock turned toward the bar and looked over his shoulder. He dropped his voice down, jokingly, to the menacing level from before. "Come on."

"After you," Drake motioned for Cleo to fall in behind Rock. "It looks like we're being summoned."

Rock looked comfortable behind the bar and he motioned for Cleo and Drake to climb on the barstools in front of him. "So whatta-lit-be?" Rock asked as he scooped ice into a glass. When he set the glass on the bar mat, glittering chunks of frozen water splattered onto the work surface in front ɔf him.

"The usual, Ms. Martin?" When she nodded, Rock picked up the beverage gun and pressed a button, causing a stream of dark liquid to fill the ice-filled glass in front of him. When it was almost completely filled, Rock depressed a different button and a clear liquid topped off the glass. Next he picked up a straw and stirred the drink before placing it on a cocktail napkin and sliding it in front of Cleo.

"Oh, wait. A garnish of lemon." Rock plopped a wedge of lemon into the drink, causing a mini tidal wave. "I don't know why Kevin won't hire me as a bartender. I think I'm the epitome of grace and style when it comes to making drinks."

Rock scooped another glass into the ice container in front of him. "Whatta-lit-be, Drake? Whiskey? Vodka? Gin? Maybe some Te-qu-i-lla?" Rock sounded like he was an auctioneer or a broadcaster giving a rundown of a horse race. Cleo couldn't decide which.

She wondered what type of drink Drake liked. He looked like a "shaken, not stirred" kinda guy.

"I'll have what she's having." Drake motioned towards Cleo's drink. More ice clattered onto the work space as Rock busied himself putting together another drink.

"By the way, what are you having?" Drake turned towards Cleo.

"Sort of a modified lemon coke. Cola with a splash of 7-Up."

"Hey, don't forget the garnish." Rock scolded from behind the counter as he dropped a lime wedge into Drake's drink. "Oops. I hope you don't mind a slight variation. You just can't get good help these days."

As Rock started to prepare a drink for himself, he motioned to the video cassette on the bar. "What's that? Your commercial?" When Cleo nodded, he winked at Drake. "Mind like a steel trap." Rock paused. "Well, come on, let's pop that puppy into the VCR." On the opposite side of the bar was a wall of television monitors that greeted patrons as they entered Podium. Walking around the wall of screens exposed the bar and dance floor.

Cleo wasn't sure how she felt about viewing her commercial in front of Drake and Rock. She wanted to curl up in her bed, cozy and safe as she watched. The twenty TV screens at Podium presented an overwhelming opportunity.

"Have you seen this yet, Drake?" Rock asked as he walked over to the VCR and popped out the current tape.

"Yes, I have."

Well, Cleo felt comfortable with Rock and Drake had already seen it. It would probably be alright to view it here. Several of the other dancers had already arrived but they were back in the dressing room.

"Split screen or individual?" Rock was busy setting up the VCR. It was possible to have the TV screens show twenty repetitive images or one-twentieth of the screen to give a large screen illusion. "I know, let's watch it both ways."

Cleo knew that Rock would not push the issue if she vocalized a request not to view the commercial but curiosity was getting the better of her. She wanted to see how everything fit together. She had no control over the fact that the commercial would be going national in several days, whether she liked the work or not.

Rock reached out and held his hand open for the video cassette in Cleo's grasp. She extended her arm and Rock took the cassette from her. She watched, almost as if everything was moving in slow motion as Rock pushed the tape into the VCR. Cleo slid off the bar stool and walked around to the other side to watch the screens in front of her. The monitors in front of her were blank and fuzzy while Rock queued up the video. As the tape started to hum and the countdown picture appeared, Cleo held her breath.

CHAPTER FIVE

"Healthy Shine Commercial...Sixty Seconds...The Stockton Agency."

Cleo watched and listened as the dark grey screens in front of her changed to a film leader counting down to the beginning of the commercial. When it started, the locations were familiar but the images caught her off-guard. She could hardly believe her eyes. Was that really her?

"Healthy Shine...Shampoo and conditioner in one...Save time...Do what you want..."

Cleo recognized her voice from the studio shoot. Dance music played in the background as a flurry of images flashed onto the screen to be replaced quickly by another and another. A whirlwind of activity flashed before her eyes. Cleo on the beach, Cleo in an office, Cleo on a merry-go-round. Finally the image of a Healthy Shine shampoo bottle bouncing on bathroom tile with a voice over; "Healthy Shine Shampoo and Conditioner...Do What You Want."

Smooth grey filled the screen again and Cleo stood in front of the monitors, stunned. Never in her wildest dreams would she have thought the fun, sparkling, vibrant woman in the commercial was her. She didn't look like that. She was the girl next door. One of the guys. Sure, she laughed and smiled but the cameras had done the trick. It had to be the work of the cameraman who had made her look the way she did. The cameraman and the make-up crew.

"Wow! Let's see it again." Rock was the first one to react. Within seconds he'd run around to the bar and reset the VCR. This time, when the commercial started, it filled each TV monitor and created a large screen image, replacing the twenty repetitive images there'd been with the first preview.

The result was overpowering and Cleo felt compelled to take several steps backwards. She brushed Drake's arm as she stepped behind. She couldn't tell what he was thinking as he watched the commercial. Looking forward again, Cleo was caught up in the flurry of images in front of her and the strong musical beat. The commercial was energizing.

Too soon the voice over was heard again and the images replaced with the cool grey of blank tape. "You'll probably think I'm biased because TSA produced the commercial, but I think it's great." Drake looked at Cleo and quietly added. "You're great."

Cleo felt extremely flustered. She wasn't ready for the intense look Drake was giving her and the images of the commercial were still replaying through her mind. She'd completely forgotten about Rock until his voice boomed between her and Drake.

"Wow, Cleo! I'm speechless and for an English major that's a rarity." Rock turned towards Drake, "Your company made this? How do you come up with the ideas?" Rock fired off a bunch of questions about the advertising components of the commercial, giving Cleo a moment to process her feelings. She was thankful the bouncer was there to take the attention away from her.

"Hey, Rock, I thought you said you were speechless." Cleo laughed as she watched the exchange between the two men. She was surprised to see them side by side. Rock was certainly a considerable amount taller but Drake didn't look dwarfed like so many other men did when they stood next to the hefty bouncer.

Drake highlighted the creative process for Rock, everything from concept development to art boards, client approval to filming in a quick overview. Rock listened, fascinated as he entered the unfamiliar world of advertising.

The numbness Cleo had felt when the commercial had finished was dissipating. She realized with shock that she still needed to get ready to dance.

"Drake, thanks for bringing the commercial by." She started to walk backwards towards the dressing room. "TSA did an amazing job. I'm sure your client will be thrilled."

"Randy loved it. He can't place where he knows you from. He thinks you did a photo layout or something."

"Randy?"

"Yeah, Randy. He's the Marketing Director at Carlisle Corporation, the makers of Healthy Shine."

"Randy?" Cleo was stunned. "From that night here?"

"Yeah, kind of ironic, huh?"

"I made a commercial for the company Randy works for?" Cleo was having trouble assimilating the news. How should she feel? She didn't know if she should be angry or giddy.

"Hey, was that the creep you told me about?" When Cleo shook her head affirmatively, Rock growled. "It still makes me mad I was bringing kegs up to the bar and missed him. I would've liked to have shown that guy the door."

"Its okay, Rock. It didn't turn nasty like some of the other situations we've had."

Drake looked embarrassed and Cleo was concerned he might get the wrong idea. "Rock's very protective of the dancers. Usually no one's even able to get near us. Randy was mild, don't even worry about it."

"What other types of situations have you had?"

Rock started to laugh. "Remember that guy who jumped up on the pedestal with Ju-Dee and tried to do 'The Bump' with her? He was so drunk she 'bumped' him right off. Good thing his friends were there to break his fall."

"What's happened to you, Cleo?"

"Situations like the time with Randy are about it." Drake looked skeptical. "Really, don't worry. Rock takes care of me."

"She's right, Drake. No one gets near the dancers for any length of time and no one has ever been hurt." Rock laughed again. "Well, no one except the ones who get scraped as they hit the pavement outside."

"I wouldn't be dancing here if I didn't think it was safe," Cleo interjected.

Rock looked serious. "Podium has a high-class image to maintain. If someone's looking for a strip show they should try one of the clubs on Western."

Drake looked relieved. "You're right, Podium's a nice club. I didn't see anything, other than Randy's behavior, to indicate otherwise."

"Well, I'm really running late. The dressing room calls."

Cleo held out her hand. "Thanks again. Bye, Drake."

Drake took her hand gently. "Bye, Cleo."

❧

Well, that was it, Cleo chided herself as she pulled a brush through her hair. "Bye, Cleo." was pretty finite. Over the course of a brief encounter she was feeling a plethora of emotions. Excitement about the commercial. Uncertainty about it being for the company Randy worked for. Confusion about Drake.

Cleo put the hairbrush down as she realized she was brushing so hard her scalp hurt. The bottom line – the commercial was great. She wasn't sure how she ended up looking so good but it was fun and energetic and she'd had a blast filming it.

Did it matter that the company who promoted Healthy Shine Shampoo & Conditioner had Randy as their Marketing Director? No, definitely not. In a way, Drake was right. It was ironic that Randy was paying her money for being in his commercial and he couldn't even place her as the pedestal dancer at Podium.

It was easy to resolve her problems talking to herself in front of the mirror. But what about Drake Stockton? He'd said goodbye. Did that mean he was gone for good? It was nice that he'd been concerned for her safety while she danced at the club. He almost seemed paternal in his protective-ness. Cleo was glad he'd agreed that Podium was respectable. Even several of the dancers were men so it really wasn't fair to parallel it to a bar with nude dancers.

Looking at her watch she realized she'd been caught up in her own thoughts for way too long. She needed to hurry if she wanted to be ready to dance on time.

Cleo dressed quickly in her club attire and made her way out to the dance floor to take her place on one of the front pedestals. Normally she was able to remove herself from the crowded room and find a mental escape while she was dancing. She almost fell off her pedestal when she looked over and saw Drake sitting on one of the bar stools. How disconcerting to see him here. Hadn't he said goodbye?

It felt both alarming and comfortable to have him watching over her. She replayed the conversation they'd had right before she'd gone to the dressing room and she was sure he was still here out of concern. Rock had been right. Most of the time, patrons of the club were harmless. Only on rare occasions did things take an ugly turn.

The calls she had been receiving were rude and crude but Cleo didn't believe they were connected in any way to the club. The caller seemed to have dialed her phone number at random. He'd never used her name or referenced anything personal about her. He'd only been candid about what he wanted her to do to him. She always hung up the phone without making any response, so she'd only heard his first identifying comments.

Cleo caught Drake's gaze from across the room and her eyes didn't leave his for a long pause while she gyrated atop the small dance space. She felt as if his eyes were able to bore into the center of her soul and she finally turned on the pedestal to get away from his penetrating stare. There was nothing sexual in the way he looked at her but his gaze was certainly possessive, assuring her no one would be able to touch her.

When she turned again to face him, Cleo was relieved to see Rock had engaged him in conversation, momentarily distracting him. She danced for the entire evening with Drake sitting on a bar stool, protectively observing her and the patrons at Podium. Cleo found it comforting and soothing to have Drake as an added Guardian Angel and Rock didn't seem to mind.

They were able to speak briefly while Cleo was on her breaks and then he resumed his watchful position at the bar. Drake was very brotherly in his approach towards her and only conveyed concern. He'd never passed judgement about her dancing as so many other men she met had felt compelled to do. Most men didn't seem to understand. They immediately thought it was like dancing at a topless bar. The two worlds couldn't have been further apart.

Drake had been a true gentleman throughout the entire evening and Rock even allowed him to stay as they were closing the bar but he walked with both of them as they made their way into the parking lot.

Drake had looked puzzled at first when Cleo exited the dressing room with her helmet in hand. She smiled. She'd deposited her bag and helmet before seeing Drake earlier. When they walked into the nearly empty parking lot she headed towards her motorcycle, parked against the side of the building.

She waited for Drake to make the typical response she got when most people discovered she rode a motorcycle. It didn't come. She glanced over to see his expression.

Drake smiled. "I don't know why, but it fits."

"Do you want to go for a ride?" Cleo couldn't help but tease him.

"I guess that depends if I'm on in the front or the back."

"Don't you trust me?"

"I don't know."

"Don't worry, you weigh too much anyway. I'd have trouble keeping the bike centered if you were on the back."

"That's funny, I never thought of myself as being too heavy." Drake's rich, deep laugh filled the still evening air.

Cleo thought he looked like the perfect amount of muscle -- not too much and not too little.

"Okay, then it's settled. I'll ride in the front. Ready?"

Cleo's laugh caught in her throat. "Do you know how to ride a motorcycle?"

"Yup. Get on, let's go."

"But I don't have an extra helmet."

"That's okay. There's not a lot of traffic this time of night."

Cleo wasn't sure how she felt about straddling the imposing Drake Stockton from behind but going for a night ride with him certainly seemed appealing.

"Okay, let's go." Cleo tossed the keys towards Drake and they glinted in the moonlight as they sailed through the air.

Cleo had forgotten Rock was still with them until his voice boomed in her ear. "Are you guys really going for a ride now?" Cleo nodded as she pulled on her helmet. "Well then, wait here." Rock jogged the short distance to his car and pulled out a helmet designed for off-road terrain. "I went riding up in the mountains this last weekend with some friends. Lucky for you, the helmet's still in the car."

Drake took the helmet Rock handed him and nodded appreciatively. "Thanks."

"Yeah, no problem. Leave it with Cleo and she can return it to me tomorrow."

"Nice meeting you, Rock."

"Hey, you too, Drake."

It was as wonderful as Cleo could have imagined to wrap herself around the strong body of the man in front of her. He hadn't been lying when he said he knew how to ride and he handled the bike easily.

Cleo didn't know how long they rode but she enjoyed every minute. The air was cool and luxuriously lapped over them as they wound up into the hills above Hollywood along Mulholland Drive.

The evening was unusually crystal clear and the lights of the city blinked and shimmered below them. Cleo thought it was hard to imagine how many people actually lived in Los Angeles. Looking at the lights that spread out for miles it was easy to see why the neighboring suburbs merged together and added to the enormity of the popula-population.

Drake pulled the bike over to the side of the road and turned off the engine. Cleo felt like she was back in high school, being taken to the local make-out location. It was early enough in the morning that there were no other vehicles around but Cleo knew this area of Mulholland attracted the romantics of Los Angeles.

They both un-straddled the bike and walked slowly down Mulholland until they found a flat surface with an unobstructed view of the world around them.

"Isn't the city beautiful?" Drake sighed contentedly as he looked out at the twinkling lights. "I've always loved Los Angeles."

"Me, too. I can't imagine where else I'd rather live."

"Funny isn't it?, considering the reputation."

"I don't mind the rep. If people want to live somewhere else maybe the freeway system will run smoother."

Drake laughed and the deep rich tones carried in the still evening air. "I don't know if we'll ever be that lucky."

They sat in silence for a while, listening to the subtle sounds of the nearly quiet city below. The air was crisp and clean and the desert around them smelled dry and prickly.

Cleo could feel the warmth of Drake's body next to her and she wanted to lean closer to touch what she could feel and absorb the heat he was radiating. She wondered if he felt the same current that seemed to be passing between them.

What was she going to do about her feelings? Luckily the commercial was completed. At least she wouldn't have to consider the implications if there was still work to be done. Cleo felt very strongly about not mixing work and play. And boy, was she sure getting the urge to play right now. She wanted to reach over and touch the man next to her. She wanted to see if his chest was as firm as she anticipated it to be. She wanted to be wrapped in his arms and protected from the world. Looking at the lights below, it was hard to imagine the city could be threatening and imposing and yet Cleo wanted to feel the strength and safety of his arms around her.

The dry desert grass around her provided enough distraction. It was easier to rip the grass out of the ground than rip the clothes off Drake's body. Besides, she'd always been taught that wasn't lady like. She wondered why she was getting the urge right now since it wasn't her normal mode of behavior.

❦

Drake looked over at Cleo and watched as she plucked the slender reeds of grass out of the ground around them. She seemed nervous. He hoped he didn't frighten her. He guessed the evening had been rather unorthodox so far. He'd only planned on dropping off the copy of the commercial and heading home.

Never in his wildest dreams did he think he would stay at the club for over five hours. God, had it really been that long? He'd felt captivated watching Cleo dance and he'd admired how she'd handled the other patrons of Podium. He'd felt a need to protect her -- but for the life of him he couldn't figure out why. She had shown him she was very capable.

She was so beautiful. He was having a hard time putting thoughts of her out of his mind. Thoughts of throwing her down on the ground and enjoying every inch of her. He'd been raised to respect women. He was feeling very much like Hannibal Lecter telling Clarissa, "All good things to those who wait." Great. Nothing like comparing yourself to a serial killer. And a fictional one at that.

Cleo turned towards him and that's when he knew. He wasn't going to be patient. He wasn't going to be able to wait. He pulled her roughly against his chest and bent his head in search of her mouth.

๛

He was firm and gentle as he took her into his arms. As he kissed her she tried to lean closer, savor the taste of him, the smell of him. His mouth was teasing and tempting her in ways she could never have anticipated. Their tongues met and explored. Her breathing became short and she gasped, trying to pull oxygen into her lungs and re-stabilize her shaky equilibrium.

She wondered if he was as well rehearsed in other arenas. He certainly seemed like the type of man who knew women very well. Almost too well. She didn't want to respond to him this way. It was too easy to fall into the illusion around them and she refused to be a sucker. There was too much to lose. Cleo placed her hands on his firm, muscular chest and enjoyed the heat of his skin for a moment before pushing him away.

"Thanks, but no thanks." Cleo stood up and brushed the loose leaves of grass from her jeans. "Been there, done that." *What could she have been thinking? Why hadn't it occurred to her that a moonlit bike ride with Drake Stockton would lead to this?* It occurred to Cleo that she'd developed a false sense of security by convincing herself that Drake Stockton wasn't interested in her as a woman, only as an actress. She should've been smarter than that.

"You know, some people would say that kissing someone is very natural and normal." Drake's voice was deep and clear behind her. "Kind of a nice way of letting someone know you like them."

"Yeah, but it doesn't fit into my life right now. I'm not looking for a relationship..." Cleo paused as she contemplated the extent of what Drake had been offering. "Or a one-night stand...Or a month long fling. Whatever you want to call it."

"Okay." Drake said the word slowly and Cleo realized the extent of his arousal. "How about a friend, Cleo? Are you able to fit a friend into your life right now?"

"Yeah, I guess so."

"Friends." Drake extended his hand.

Cleo took his hand and shook it firmly once. "Friends."

❧

"Hi, Mrs. Richards!" Cleo waved to her elderly landlady who was kneeling alongside one of her glorious flower beds.

"Cleo, dear, how're you this morning?" Lorna Richards was a slight, motherly woman who lived in the main house in front of Cleo's cottage apartment. "I saw the commercial you were in, dear, and you looked lovely. Simply lovely."

The commercial had been airing for a week and many of Cleo's friends and family had seen it. Everyone at the club had been giving her a hard time about her "star" quality, joking about rolling out the red carpet.

"I'm glad you liked the commercial, Mrs. Richards. I really had a lot of fun filming it."

"You look like you're off on another adventure, dear." Mrs. Richards motioned towards the helmet and black bag Cleo was carrying.

Cleo smiled. "Actually, I'm off to another audition."

"Aah, to be young. How exciting. Is this for another commercial?"

"No, not today. I'm going on a second reading for a feature film." Cleo's nerves were stretched, thinking about the audition. She'd been surprised and thrilled to get the call back on the Meyerson film. She'd have to keep her fingers crossed and hope for the best. She tried to distance herself from the strong emotions she'd felt when she first read the script.

"Well, break a leg, dear." Mrs Richards scooped up a mound of earth with a hand trowel and picked up a potted petunia. She meticulously removed the flower with the cube of dirt attached to the roots and placed it into the indentation she'd just made. Quickly she worked the loose soil in place around the petunia. Cleo watched as she repeated the motions to create a border along the wall of the flower bed.

"Thanks Mrs. Richards. I'll see you later." Cleo waved again as she climbed onto her bike and pulled on her helmet. It didn't take her long to reach Laurel Canyon and start the winding trek through the canyon.

As she wove her way towards Burbank to audition, Cleo pushed the nervous thoughts she'd had about the impending interview from her mind. She wanted to be fresh and unencumbered before she arrived. The cool breeze washed over her face and she was thankful she didn't have a visor on her helmet so she could enjoy the smells of the canyon. Wild flowers and grasses grew throughout the canyon between the scattered array of homes.

Laurel Canyon had an odd mixture of buildings. Everything from a mansion that was rumored to have belonged to the great magician, Houdini, to small buildings that looked like decrepit shacks ready to fall down. The canyon was a haven for artists and successful business people looking for a quiet retreat. Jim Morrison was even rumored to have lived in a house near the canyon market.

It didn't take long to reach her destination. After informing the casting director that she'd arrived she found a seat and pulled out the sides she was to read. She'd worked and re-worked the scene for the last several days and knew every word on the script. Re-reading it now gave her something to do, something to focus on.

"Cleo Martin! We're ready for you." A thin, young man who was assisting motioned her towards the room to read.

The reading went well. Cleo knew her part and felt confident in the choices she made to execute the character properly. Hopefully, the director had the same ideas.

"Thank you, that was very nice." A burly woman, sitting with a cigarette with ash dangling from the tip dismissed her from the reading.

Nice. The kiss of death.

"We'll be in touch with your agent..." she shuffled through the pile of papers in front of her, "...Raymond... if we're interested."

"Thank you."

"Oh, by the way, please leave your sides with the assistant outside." The burly woman never lifted her head from the pile of papers in front of her.

As Cleo climbed onto her motorcycle and revved the engine to life she tried to squelch the growing feeling of disappointment she felt flaring inside. *Hey, it isn't over until the fat lady sings.* Cleo tried to console herself as she pulled out into traffic. Well, the fat lady may not have sung yet but she definitely seemed to be warming up.

Well, that was it. The only audition she had today and there were several hours before she had to report to the club. The best thing to do would be to head home and pamper herself for the afternoon. Maybe do a little gardening. Maybe read a book. Just as long as the afternoon was lazy and relaxing. Best to put the audition behind her.

As Cleo pulled into the driveway leading to her cottage she looked for Mrs. Richards. Apparently she'd finished her own gardening and she was nowhere to be seen and the petunias were all in place and freshly watered. She parked her bike and pulled off her helmet. As she walked to the door she considered her options for the afternoon. Maybe it would be fun to wander to a movie theater and binge on matinees and popcorn.

Yeah, that was it, a little movie-marathon. Cleo was so intent on making her afternoon plans she almost tripped over the bouquet of pale pink tulips on her doorstep.

CHAPTER SIX

The tulips were gorgeous. Delicate, pearl pink buds were just beginning to open and they were tied together with a ribbon, along with a note. Cleo wondered who'd left them. God, I hope it isn't that creep, Larry. She'd had more than enough of him the night they'd gone out and she hoped he felt the same way.

She picked up the flowers and pushed through her front door, dropping her helmet and black satchel as soon as she was inside. She carried the tulips to her dining table and placed them gently on the surface and undid the ribbon to release the note.

The paper was thick and linen-like with shiny filaments of fibers creating a slight texture. Her name was boldly written on the front with, what was that? A fountain pen? Who wrote with fountain pens these days?

Cleo pulled out a monogrammed card from inside. "DTS" was etched on the cover. Drake! Had he been there? Cleo wondered what the "T" stood for as she opened the note.

"I saw these today and they reminded me of you. Here's to our new friendship. Drake."

Cleo didn't know what to think. Flowers meant more than friendship didn't they? But his note acknowledged their conversation. They were to have nothing more than a friendship.

It was several hours later, after two movies and lots of buttered popcorn, when Cleo pushed open the door to Podium and stepped into the darkened entrance.

"Hey woman!," Cleo greeted Ju-Dee as she entered the dressing room.

"Girl, you sit your pretty little butt in that chair and tell me what happened last night. First that perfectly delicious Drake Stockton shows up and never leaves. Then you ride off with him. I'd say you rode into the sunset but it was the middle of the night."

"It sounds like you already know the story."

"Hell, girl, the story started when you left. Spill it. And don't leave out a single detail."

Cleo laughed. It was just like her friend to push her into a corner. "You already know most of it. We rode up along Mulholland and then we came back here and I dropped him at his car."

"That's it? He doesn't strike me as the type of man who'd settle for a handshake at the door -- not that I'd want him to." Ju-Dee winked at Cleo.

"I'll let him know you said so."

"Yeah, right. I don't need glasses to see that he didn't take his eyes off of you all night."

Cleo could feel the color rising in her cheeks and she was glad Ju-Dee was the only one around. "We're friends, Ju-Dee, nothing more."

"As I said before...yeah, right."

"He sent me flowers today and his note even acknowledged that we're just friends."

"Whoa, whoa, stop right there. He sent you flowers?"

Cleo opened her organizer and pulled out the card from Drake and handed it to Ju-Dee. "Read it -- you'll see."

"As a friend of mine once told me, don't listen to what a man says, listen to what a man does. He may be saying he wants to be your friend but what he's doing seems to say a whole lot more."

"You're kidding, right?" Cleo felt panic rising inside of her. She wasn't ready for anything more than a friendship with Drake Stockton. She wasn't sure if she'd ever be ready for anything else with him.

Ju-Dee must have sensed her anxiety. "What kind of flowers were they?"

"Pale, pink tulips." Cleo answered, her mind racing miles away.

"Oh, well, that's different than red roses. Don't worry about it. I'm sure everything's fine."

"I was very clear with him, Ju-Dee."

"I'm sure you were, honey. His note's right."

"What do you mean?"

"Pale, pink tulips do seem to suit you. I like him. Drake is a decent guy from what I can tell."

"Yeah, I think you're right." Secretly, Cleo hoped Ju-Dee was right.

❧

"Paychecks! Paychecks!" Rock's voice boomed through the air. "Line up, let's go, let's go."

"Hey, Rock, are you sure you're not in ROTC? You're like a crazy drill sergeant."

"Flattery won't get you anywhere." Rock waved a bunch of envelopes in the air. "And, it won't get you your paycheck any sooner. They're in random order."

Rock started roll-call. Cleo watched as the members of her extended family interacted around her. She was so absorbed she almost missed her own name when Rock called which was surprising since he was rather loud in delivery.

She opened the envelope and peered at the check inside. The usual. No surprises but it felt good to get paid. It was a sense of security knowing she could pay her rent and eat a decent meal. Her expenses were minimal and she enjoyed supporting herself.

She knew a lot of people would consider her pay from Podium as insignificant but she didn't need much more. For the most part, she felt her life was complete. Sometimes she wished she could freeze-frame everything so she could enjoy this time. She knew it wouldn't last and she hoped to hold onto it for as long as she could.

"Hey, Cleo, do you want to go bowling with us Saturday afternoon? A group of us are getting together in Studio City to bowl and nosh." Rock's voice bellowed across the room. There was a bowlng alley in the Valley with a traditional deli next door. A person really hadn't lived until they blended the interesting experience of bowling and pastrami on rye. It wasn't expected and yet it worked.

"That sounds great. Let me make sure I'm free." Cleo pulled out her organizer and scanned her calendar. "What time?"

"We're going to meet at the deli at noon and bowl afterwards."

Cleo penciled in the information and closed her book. "It's a done deal. Do you want to carpool?"

"Yeah, we'll work something out. Right now there are about seven of us. We'll probably have to take two cars as it is."

Ju-Dee slid up next to Cleo and whispered in her ear. "Why don't you ask Drake Stockton if he wants to come?"

Cleo had to suppress a laugh. What would Drake think if she asked him bowling? The thought of Mr. Designer Suits in rented bowling shoes was somewhat comical. Well, he'd been right at home at Carney's so maybe it would be alright. Besides, how was she going to emphasize that they were just to be friends if they didn't do anything together?

Cleo tried not to think about the fact that it sounded like she was trying to rationalize calling him to get together.

❧

As she paced around her small apartment shortly before noon on Saturday, she remembered the phone call she'd made to Drake earlier in the week.

"So you'll go?" Cleo had tried to keep the incredulous tone out of her voice.

"Yeah, it sounds like fun." Drake's rich, deep voice answered her across the phone line and Cleo realized that she'd convinced herself he would say no.

"Do you want me to pick you up at eleven forty-five Saturday?" Drake's voice had broken through her shell-shocked state of mind.

"What? Oh, sure. That would be fine."

Now she found herself pacing as she waited for Drake to arrive. Considering they were only supposed to be friends, the afternoon get-together was suddenly beginning to feel like a date.

Since she hardly ever drank, Cleo thought it was funny she was almost craving a shot of something to calm her nerves. Hell, she was an actress, she could get through this. But she realized there was a big difference between life and acting.

In life you were given "take one" with no opportunity to try again if you didn't get it right. Acting allowed you to try and try again until you got the desired result. That wasn't to say that you couldn't learn through your mistakes in life but the out-takes weren't so easily disposed of as they were in an editor's cutting room.

What was she thinking anyway? It was an afternoon of bowling. Taking a ball that was usually too heavy and drilled for somebody else's hand and hurling it towards ten pins while wearing two-toned shoes that many people had worn before. No big deal. Bowling.

Cleo looked down at her oversized blue chambray shirt with "Ned" embroidered on the pocket and wondered if she had time to change. With the white tank top and jeans she was also wearing she looked like she could have worked at the service station where Ned had, if there ever had been a Ned. In fact, Cleo had bought the shirt new at a Melrose boutique because she thought it was comfortable and fun. Now she wasn't quite so sure. It was feeling more and more like a date as the minutes ticked by.

Cleo had started her pacing well before Drake Stockton was due to arrive and when he drove into her driveway she was surprised to notice it was only two minutes past the agreed upon time. By Los Angeles standards that was very much on time since traffic was never predictable.

She grabbed her large satchel bag and was out the door before Drake had an opportunity to park his car. She waved to him before she turned to lock the front door and she realized her heart was pounding and her breathing was shallow. She took two deep breaths before she turned to greet Drake properly.

He had gotten out of his car and walked around to the passenger's side and was holding the door open for her. The top was down and Cleo could hear subtle strains of music coming from the interior of the car.

A light breeze caught her hair and lifted it slightly off of her shoulders as she walked toward the open car door. Everything seemed to be moving in slow motion as she slid into the car and Drake closed the door behind her.

"The bowling alley is on Ventura Boulevard. The easiest way to get there is over Laurel Canyon."

"Okay, but I'm not leaving until you have your seat belt on." Drake leaned across Cleo and grasped the belt in his hand and passed it to Cleo. "Car rules."

Cleo could smell his aftershave as he brushed in front of her and she realized she wanted lean closer and inhale deeply. So much for self control.

After she was buckled in safely, she watched Drake put the car in reverse and back out of her driveway. She had been so intent on getting into the car she hadn't noticed what Drake was wearing.

She was reminded of the night that she'd mentally created a "Drake doll" and dressed him in a variety of styles when she realized that he was wearing a pair of blue jeans which were nicely faded like the image she'd had in her mind's eye. He was also wearing a rugby shirt and Doc Martens that transformed him from the Advertising Executive he was during the week to the weekend boy-next-door. Funny though, Cleo would never have thought of him as the boy-next-door type. He still had an aura of authority around him that even the clothes couldn't diffuse.

"Thanks again for the tulips. They were beautiful."

"You're welcome. I'm glad you enjoyed them."

"Drake, what does the "T" stand for?"

"What "T"?"

"The one on your card. You know, the "T" for your middle name?"

Drake laughed. "Oh, that "T". It stands for Trent."

"Drake Trent Stockton. I like it."

"Trent is actually my father's first name and Drake is my mother's maiden name. She insisted that her maiden name get carried down in one way or another so they picked it to be my first name."

"I wondered about that. I don't think I've ever met anyone with the first name Drake."

"Yeah, about as often as you meet someone named Cleo."

She laughed. "I was named for my grandmother. She always loved Cleopatra and even played her part on stage in New York. My mom finally agreed to name me Cleo for her mother."

"In my line of work we actually have an award with your name. It's spelled a little differently but it's pronounced the same."

"How's it spelled?"

"C-L-I-O."

"What's it for?"

"It recognizes the best advertising in the world. I guess you could say it's my world's equivalent to your world's Oscar."

"Have you ever won one?"

"Not yet, but we keep trying."

"I'm sure you'll get one someday."

Drake pulled up to a red light at Ventura Boulevard and turned towards Cleo. "Which way?"

"Left. It's not too far down on the right hand side. I'll point it out to you."

As they pulled into the parking lot for the bowling alley and deli, Drake glanced towards Cleo. "You make a good navigator."

"Thanks. You make a good driver."

"Yeah, I think we make a pretty good team."

Oh, God, it felt like a date again.

The rest of the group was easy to find. Rock, as usual, had been the first to arrive and had staked out a large table in the corner. Cleo waved to him as they approached. Ju-Dee and Tracey, another dancer, had already arrived and Cleo introduced Drake after they slid into their seats.

"Paula couldn't make it but Cliff and Stan should be here soon," Rock informed the group as they scanned their menus. With the exception of Drake, the rest of the group all worked at Podium. Cleo wondered how he would fit in and if he would like her extended family. In many ways, this would be a harder initiation than if she had actually taken him home to meet her parents.

The meal went well and Cleo began to relax. She enjoyed watching Drake as he interacted with the group around him. Her first impression had been that he was a powerful man, comfortable in his world of big business. Here, at the deli, he showed an uncanny ability to shed his other skin and be like any of the people around him. It would be interesting to see what happened when they started bowling. Would he continue to be the chameleon or would he return to the man of business, unable to infiltrate into this social setting. Without realizing it, Cleo was testing the man with her. Testing if he was who he appeared to be with her. Testing if he would be able to fit into her life.

After the last of the dishes had been removed and a flurry of money had been tossed onto the table to cover the bill, Rock stood up and bellowed, "You guys ready to BOWL?"

Cheers and whistles erupted from the group.

"Let's go!"

Cleo slid from the booth and slipped beside Drake who waited for her. She could feel the firm touch of his hand on the small of her back as they walked towards the bowling alley entrance. She wanted to press backwards, into his hand. She wanted him to protect her. She felt safe and secure with him by her side.

"Okay, I've reserved lanes four and five. Get your shoes and meet me over there!" Rock brandished his bowling ball and turned towards the lanes.

Drake turned towards her. "What size shoes do you need?"

"Seven"

"Great, I'll get our shoes. Do you want to start looking for a bowling ball?"

"Sure. I'll meet you over by the lanes."

Cleo wandered along the rows of alley provided bowling balls, trying to find a ball that was light enough and drilled to accommodate her fingers. The majority of the balls were black and she gravitated towards the bright colored ones that were dispersed throughout. It didn't take her long to locate a marbleized, pink colored ball that felt comfortable. As she carried it towards the group she watched Drake at the front counter and almost collided with Ju-Dee.

"I caught you!" Ju-Dee ribbed her friend good-naturedly. "If I wasn't already involved with someone, I'd be looking, too!"

Warmth spread across Cleo's face as she turned towards Ju-Dee, ready to deny everything. As she could feel the warmth grow hotter on her cheeks she thought better of saying anything regarding Drake. "Which lane are you bowling on?"

"Five. Cliff, Stan, Tracey and I have already staked claim. You and Drake are bowling with Rock on lane four."

The two lanes shared a ball return so they weren't far from one another. Cleo realized she was thankful for the company of her friends. Being around Drake when it was just the two of them could be disconcerting.

"Here are your shoes, Cleo." Drake was holding out a pair of two-toned shoes towards her. "I'll be back. I'm going to pick out a ball."

Ju-Dee leaned towards Cleo after Drake walked out of hearing range. "Actually, a little looking didn't hurt anyone. Don't worry, I promise not to touch."

Possessiveness flared unexpectedly inside Cleo, catching her off-guard. She and Drake were going to be friends, nothing more. Just because the day was feeling more and more like a date didn't change their conversation. Friends. They'd even shook on it, making it official.

"Ready to get serious?" Rock's head was bent intently as he scribbled down their names on the score sheet. He looked up and met Cleo's eyes. "Go ahead, try a couple practice shots to get used to your ball."

Cleo stood at the foot of the lane, holding her ball with both hands. She tried to remind herself of the proper way to hold the ball, the steps she would take as she pulled the ball behind her and the crouching position to assume when she brought the ball forward and released it. She reminded herself to keep her wrist straight when she released the ball to avoid spinning the ball into the gutter.

Three strides forward, down and release. She watched as the ball spiraled down the alley. She would have to adjust for the ball being drilled for someone else but as she watched eight pins fall she decided the ball was going to be alright.

She turned back towards the ball return and waited for her ball to spew from the cavern below. She knew Drake had returned before she turned to face the group. Something about Drake Stockton always triggered a response, alerting her to his presence.

It was surprising how first impressions of a person could omit so much about them. Drake was everything that Cleo had expected him to be upon their first meeting – competent, strong and dependable. What she hadn't expected was for him to be such a good bowler.

They'd played several frames when Drake assumed his position, getting ready to throw the ball.

"Drake, if you get this strike, that will be three in a row." Rock winked at Cleo. "I'm trying to apply a little pressure."

"You're not breaking my concentration, Rock – sorry." Drake started towards the front line. Both lanes stopped to watch as the ball sped down the lane towards the ten pins. Upon impact the pins clattered and splayed. None of the pins were left standing.

"You did it!" Rock patted him on the back and laughed. "You know what that means, don't you?"

"It means I'm ahead by eight points."

Cleo watched the two men in front of her. They interacted like they had known each other for years.

"Actually, Drake, it's a turkey," Rock explained. "It also means you buy the group a round of drinks. House rules!"

"Liar!" Cleo laughed as she interrupted. "It means we have to buy him a drink, Rock."

"Shhh, Cleo. I figured buying us drinks might incentivize the bowling master here to lighten up a little bit." Rock put his arm around Cleo's shoulders. "You didn't tell me you were bringing a ringer with you."

"Are you saying we don't give you good competition normally, Rock? Somehow I almost feel insulted." Cleo feigned dismay and turned towards Drake. "I've always had to rely on the kindness of strangers," she crooned in a southern accent, quoting the play by Tennessee Williams.

"What would you like to drink?" Rock turned towards Drake. "I'm buying in honor of your turkey."

The group of bowlers yelled out their orders to Rock and he bounded towards the cafeteria. Tracey followed closely behind to help him carry the drinks back to the lanes.

"I'm having a lot of fun. Thanks for inviting me." Drake's voice brushed against her ear from behind and she realized how close he was standing to her.

"I'm glad." Cleo turned to look at his face and she could feel her cheeks begin to warm as she looked into his eyes. Why did this afternoon feel like a date? She didn't want to explore why she wished it was.

"Is it my turn to bowl?" She tried to break the connection between them as she used a bowling towel to wipe her ball. It felt heavy and awkward in her hands and she tried to concentrate on her footing.

Overall the afternoon was enjoyable. Drake and Rock had already met and interacted as if they had known each other for years and the rest of the group welcomed Drake effortlessly as well. Cleo was thankful that the initiation had been easy and painless.

"Ready to call it a day?" Drake looked at Cleo expectantly.

"Yeah. I don't think I have the energy to lift that ball one more time."

"Did you want to grab a bite to eat on the way home?"

Cleo liked the way that sounded as Drake said it. Home.

"I don't think I could eat anything else. Rock kept bringing things to nibble on all afternoon."

Cleo looked at the man beside her. "Are you really hungry?"

"No. I just didn't want the day to end just yet and food was the first thing I could think of as a way to prolong our time together."

She didn't want the day to end yet either. "I've got an idea. Why don't we go to a movie and eat a popcorn supper."

"Perfect."

"Do you mind if we drive to my house first. I'd like to get a jacket and I've got the daily paper so we can check the movie listings."

"Sounds like a plan. Let's go."

They discussed several of the currently released films as they made the quick drive to Cleo's apartment. They both liked the same types of movies. The day had been unexpected and it looked like the evening was going to be even better.

Cleo snuggled into the soft leather seat of Drake's car and watched him maneuver the vehicle through the twists and turns of Laurel Canyon. The afternoon had been fun.

The sun was beginning to set as Cleo unlocked her front door. Drake's tall build filled her doorway as he followed her into her home and she was reminded again of how powerful and strong he was. She flipped on the light switch located by the front door to dispel the shadows of the early evening. The light cast a soft glow throughout the room.

"The paper's on the coffee table. Why don't you find the calendar section while I get a jacket."

Cleo tried to subtly observe Drake as he walked into her home. What would he think of the way she lived? It just occurred to her that his home must be very different. After all, she was a struggling actress and Drake didn't appear to be struggling at all.

It didn't bother her, living the way she did. She just hoped her impression of Drake Stockton hadn't been wrong. Please don't let him be a materialistic kind of guy. That would be too disappointing. It was one thing to have success and abil-ability to afford material things. It was another thing entirely to have success solely for the material things it could afford.

Cleo was pleased to notice that Drake gravitated towards her personal possessions over her material things. He hesitated slightly in front of her bookcase, looking at the pictures of her family and friends that were nestled among the books and papers.

"Is this your grandmother?" Drake held the gilded frame that housed the picture of her grandmother after a New York stage production. Cleo loved that picture because it captured her grandmother doing one of the things she had enjoyed most.

"Yeah, she was a really special person."

"I can tell by the way you talk about her. The fact that you always wear the bracelet she gave you. I would have liked to have met her."

"I wish you could have, too."

Drake put the picture back on the shelf and turned his attention to the calendar listing.

"Hey, the latest Bill Meyerson film is playing in Westwood. How does that sound?"

Cleo hadn't told Drake about her auditions yet. She didn't want to do anything that might jinx her chances. She'd learned it was better not to talk about auditions because most of the time nothing materialized from her efforts.

"I'm kind of afraid to go right now."

"Why, it doesn't look like it's a scary film. It actually looks like it could be pretty funny."

"It's not that. It's just..."

"What?"

"I've auditioned twice for his next film and I don't want to get my hopes up too high. I'm afraid watching his current film will make me want the part too much. More than I already do."

"You've auditioned twice?"

"Yeah."

"That's great! Okay, we'll scratch that one off the list until you've landed the part." Drake turned the page of the calendar guide and pointed to an advertisement. "How does this look?"

Cleo looked at the colorful layout and silently thanked Drake for being so understanding. "It looks perfect."

"Okay, the next showing is in twenty-five minutes. Do you have your jacket?"

Cleo raised her hand to show the denim jacket she retrieved from her closet.

"Good, we don't want you to get sick and miss your next audition."

"I haven't even heard if I've made it to the next round yet."

"I'm sure you will. It's just a matter of time."

"Thanks for the vote of confidence. Ready?"

"Ready."

Cleo picked up her satchel and keys and pushed Drake towards the door.

Ring...Ring...Ring.

The telephone broke the silence around them.

"I'll let the machine pick it up. Let's go."

Ring...Ring...Ring.

"We've got time. Go ahead and answer it. You never know, it could be that audition call back."

Cleo dropped her things by the door and reached for the phone before the machine clicked on.

"Hello?" Her voice sounded breathy and slight as she answered the phone mid-ring.

The voice on the other end of the line was disturbing and familiar.

"Hello, Cleo. I just saw your commercial..."

CHAPTER SEVEN

The phone felt hot in Cleo's hand as she quickly slammed down the receiver. She was shaking so badly she was surprised she connected with the base of the phone. She stared at the offending contraption as if it were a snake that had just bitten her.

"What's wrong?" Drake was across the room, concern showing on his face.

"I can't believe he knows my name."

"Who? Who was that?"

"I've been getting obscene phone calls for a while. They stopped several weeks ago so I thought he'd gotten bored because I always hang up without saying anything."

"Was this the same person?"

"Yes. But this time he used my name and mentioned the commercial. Drake, that means he knows who I am, what I look like. God, he might even know where I live."

Drake's strong arms wrapped around her and his voice was soothing as he spoke, "Have you told anyone about this or contacted the police?"

"I discussed it with Rock and we both believed he'd given up. I didn't think I'd need to involve the police. Rock and I both thought he'd stopped calling."

"If he hasn't called for several weeks, I can understand why you'd be hesitant to go to the police."

Drake smoothed her hair as he spoke to her and Cleo nestled against his chest, feeling safe and secure.

"It appears to be more than a few random calls. Are you ready to go to the police to file a formal complaint? Maybe they can put a tap on your phone and trace the caller."

"I'm scared, Drake. What happens if he knows where I live? What can the police do to protect me?"

"I wouldn't worry. Let's go down to the police station and explore our options. Besides, I think I've got a solution."

"Maybe I can stay at Ju-Dee's house tonight."

"Why don't you pack an overnight bag. I know one of your friends who has a guest bedroom you can stay in tonight. After we're done at the police station, we'll worry about getting you settled."

Cleo's hands were still shaking slightly as she gathered up a nightshirt, robe and change of clothes. Cleo was thankful her small studio apartment had a walk-in closet that provided some privacy as she pushed lace panties and matching bra into her bag, along with her toothbrush and toiletry items.

It didn't take long to arrive at the West Hollywood Sheriff's Office. The desk officer was busy handing out parking permits and explaining impound charges to an irate man in his early twenties whose car had apparently been towed.

Cleo was nervous about making a statement to an officer. It seemed trivial on one hand; so far the calls had been harmless. But on the other hand, it was the first time the caller had made it personal.

Drake squeezed her hand. "How are you doing? Nervous?"

"A little. I hope they don't think I'm crazy."

"Crazy for wanting to bring an end to this creep's calls? Don't worry, they won't laugh at you. Unfortunately, I'm sure they've had this happen before."

Drake was so strong and supportive, sitting next to her. Cleo felt she could conquer anything as long as he was by her side.

"Ms. Martin? Deputy Schmidt is ready to meet with you. His desk is down this hallway." The desk deputy pointed to a doorway and Drake led the way.

The deputy was tall and thin, with sandy brown hair and wire rimmed glasses. Cleo thought he looked more like an accountant than a deputy with the Sheriff's department.

"Ms. Martin, come in and have a seat." The officer motioned to a chair in front of his desk and looked towards Drake. "Are you Mr. Martin?"

"I'm Drake Stockton, a friend of Ms. Martin's."

"Well, Mr. Stockton, I'm going to have to ask you to wait outside. Ms. Martin will be out shortly."

"I was with Ms. Martin when she received the last call and I would feel more comfortable remaining with her." Cleo was getting used to the authoritative voice that Drake used when issuing a statement.

The deputy hesitated for a moment before indicating that Drake could remain and be seated in the other chair, beside Cleo. He pulled a form from his desk drawer and made notations as Cleo spoke. She outlined the course of events over the last few months and the officer listened patiently, asking occasional questions for clarification.

After the report had been made the deputy put down his pen and looked at Drake and then Cleo. "I don't mean to sound discouraging by my next comments, but the reality is that there isn't very much we can do unless the caller calls at least three more times or if he comes forward."

"Do you mean if he comes forward and physically assaults her?" Drake's voice was edged with concern.

"Basically. But I don't want to alarm you. This type of caller enjoys his anonymity. It is very unlikely that he will ever approach Ms. Martin directly."

"Can you put a trace on her phone?" Drake leaned forward in his chair to address the officer.

"Yes, we can put a trace on the phone but unless we can record the caller three times we can't prosecute. Most people who make this type of call rotate from phone to phone to avoid problems."

"Are you telling me that there isn't a way to catch this guy?"

"No. I didn't mean to imply that this is a hopeless situation, just a difficult one. I would suggest putting a call blocking system on the phone. Each time he calls, block that number. It will make it more difficult for him to continue calling. Also, we'll need to have you start talking to him. The longer we can keep him on the phone, the better our chances are to trace the call."

"Thank you, officer, you've been very helpful," Drake said. Cleo could sense Drake's frustration.

"Sure, keep us updated if the situation changes." The deputy stood and shook their hands, dismissing them from his office.

Drake put his arm around Cleo's shoulders as they walked towards his car. "Don't worry, we'll call the phone company tomorrow and order the call blocking package."

"Drake, I appreciate your help but this is my problem. I'll call the phone company tomorrow. You don't have to worry about it."

"What are friends for if they can't help out when they are needed most?"

"You've already been very helpful. Thank you."

"No problem. Now to get you settled for the night."

"I wonder if there's a pay phone I can use." Cleo looked around the parking lot for a phone. "I want to call Ju-Dee and see if I can spend the night with her."

"I have a phone in the car you can use." Drake opened the car door and Cleo climbed into the smooth leather seat. She watched as he walked around the car and slid into the driver's seat.

He hesitated briefly, "You can call Ju-Dee if you'd like but I know the perfect place for you to stay."

"Really? Where's that?"

"At my place." Cleo could feel her jaw drop at the suggestion. "Don't worry. I've got a guest bedroom you can use. It even has a private bath. It will be like having your own private apartment."

"I can't stay at your place..."

"Why not?"

"You've already done more than enough. I can't impose on you any more than I have already."

"You're not imposing. And besides, didn't you tell me this afternoon that Ju-Dee just moved in with her boyfriend?"

"Yeah." Cleo answered hesitantly. She allowed Drake to persuade her. Ju-Dee probably would want her spending the night as much as she wanted her mother to show up unexpectedly. Maybe staying at Drake's wasn't that bad of an idea. And if she had her own private room, what harm could there be?

"It's settled, then. Shall we head home?"

Home. There that word was again. How nice it would be to make a home with the man next to her. Cleo caught herself thinking of a future with him and yet she'd been the one to limit their interactions to friendship. She didn't want to date him, did she? Why had she stopped him from pursuing her when they stopped along Mulholland Drive? Cleo remembered how she had felt when he had kissed her. Wonderful. And scared.

There's no room for romance in my life right now. No room for a relationship. I have to focus on my acting career. Cleo reminded herself.

What about passion? What's wrong with me having a fling? Cleo let out a sigh. *Because, Cleo, honey, you know you aren't cut out for the love 'em and leave 'em routine.* She knew herself too well. She'd never been a causal sex girl. Too bad.

The drive to the west side was quiet and comfortable. Drake wondered what Cleo was thinking. She hadn't said much since they'd gotten into the car and she didn't protest at being driven to his home.

She sighed as she looked out the window and Drake realized he didn't have Cleo's best interests in mind. Well, not completely anyway.

Earlier, when that creep called he'd wanted to take her into his arms and make everything better. Now he was thinking of taking her into his arms, but comforting her wasn't exactly what he had in mind.

He really enjoyed the friendship Cleo was offering him and if that was all they could have right now he'd try to be patient. But he had to be honest with himself. He wanted their friendship to be more personal. Much more personal. A naked kind of personal.

He was going to be patient. He was thirty-two years old. He could do this. He'd started his own company and was in command of a variety of projects, not to mention staff. A little thing like a libido wasn't going to be an obstacle. The only problem was that his libido was feeling anything but little.

What was she getting herself into? She felt her jaw had dropped when Drake had suggested staying at his home. Her lack of response had been taken as a positive and they'd headed on their way. In reality, Cleo had to be honest with herself. She really did like the idea.

And why not? Drake had seen where she lived. It would be interesting to see how the other half lived. The successful businessman compared to the bohemian artist. She had to giggle. Bohemian artist really wasn't accurate but it paralleled their lives accurately. He was already deeply rooted in his career and she was just beginning to dig in as an actress.

The drive had been peaceful and rhythmic and Cleo realized she had no idea where Drake lived. The Stockton Agency was located in Westwood and she'd thought that part of the city was their destination but Drake had driven through Westwood without wavering away from Wilshire Boulevard.

"I thought you lived in Westwood."

"Closer to the beach, actually."

"Oh." Again, silence. A comfortable silence that wrapped around Cleo like a blanket.

"I used to have an apartment in Westwood but I bought a house in Malibu about a year ago."

Wilshire Boulevard became a dead-end when the Pacific Ocean made it impossible to head west any further. Drake made a right turn and drove north. Soon he was pressing an electric garage door opener and a white gate surrounding a modern, white house began to open. Drake turned left and pulled his car into the semi-circular brick driveway as he waited for the gate to open wide enough to drive through.

"Well, this is where I live. You may stay here as long as you need to be safe and secure. No one will bother you here."

As Cleo climbed out of the car she was greeted by the salty smell of ocean air and she could hear the gentle lapping of the waves rolling ashore just past the house and sandy beach.

It was dark and the moon was full and illuminated the house enough for Cleo to get a feel of the architecture. Large picture windows faced the ocean. During the day she was sure the house would remind her of the pictures she'd seen of Greece with its blue sea and white sand beaches flanked by bright buildings that were her impression of the faraway county.

"Come on in." Drake led her up a few steps that opened onto a wooden deck and he unlocked one of the French doors leading into the house. Cleo looked up at the face of the building and realized there were three stories.

Drake flipped up a light switch and the soft white light filled the room. She loved the room immediately. It fit Drake, she realized, as she compared the room to his office. Both were functional and comfortable. A modern glass topped table and chairs designated a dining area in the open space. Another section of the room was divided with a plush couch and armchairs that softened the harsh lines of the modern room. A large Persian rug helped define the area. Beyond the room, Cleo could make out a patio with white and blue striped furniture and another glass table which established the beach house as a place to relax and enjoy the ocean.

"Let's put your bag in the guest room and I'll give you a quick tour."

The "guest room" was a suite located on the second level of the house. It was wonderful. Cleo felt safe and secure as she entered the spacious setting. The ocean view was visible from every window and the rhythmic sound of the waves was soothing. A large bed with a steel frame was located against one wall. It was even possible to see the ocean from the bed. Cleo wondered if she would ever want to leave the room once she'd nestled into the pillows. A variety of them were scattered at the head of the bed. Light colored paisley prints and solids blended together, creating a welcoming environment. A small, old-fashioned teddy bear was nestled into the pillows making it look like the bed came right out of a Ralph Lauren catalog.

"Here's the bathroom." Drake pushed open a doorway on the other side of the room to reveal a room that was almost as large as her apartment. There was a separate shower and a soaking tub. Everything was bright and shiny and there was a modern sink and vanity table with a basket that was filled with rolled hand towels by the sink and another basket between the shower and tub that contained larger bath sheets. There was even a phone and stereo console located on the wall closest to the doorway.

"There should be shampoo, a hair dryer, and a variety of other things in the drawers by the sink. If you don't find everything you need, let me know."

They walked back into the bedroom and Cleo noticed the alcove for the first time. A built-in settee with cushions overlooked the Pacific Ocean. The room was like an oasis.

"There's a walk-in closet over here. Feel free to unpack and make yourself comfortable."

"Drake, you have a beautiful home. Thank you for letting me stay here."

"It's really no problem. My brother, Nathan uses this room when he's in town but that's not often. It's hard to keep him in one place. Actually it's hard to keep his feet on the ground."

"What does he do?"

"He's a park ranger out on Catalina Island."

"That sounds pretty grounded to me."

"Well, he's also a pilot."

"Oh."

"Rotars can be a crazy bunch."

"Rotars?"

"Nathan's a helicopter pilot. It's a whole different breed than airplane pilots."

"He sounds like an interesting guy."

"He's a great guy. Come on, let me show you the rest of the house."

Cleo followed Drake from room to room. Each was a mix of comfort and function. Drake motioned to the stairs that led to the third level of the house. "My bedroom and study are located upstairs." Drake made no movement toward the upper rooms. Instead, he turned to walk downstairs to the first level that contained a gym and den. He showed her the living room, dining room and breakfast nook.

They ended up in the kitchen. It was the kitchen she had always dreamed of having. The refrigerator had a clear glass door which provided a view of the well-appointed interior. The stainless steel freezer filled the space to the right. A large butcher block work space was located in the center of the room and a stacked set of ovens, one standard and the other convection, were to the left of the commercial sized gas stove top. An herb garden grew on the window sill above the sink. Copper

ɔottomed pots hung from the ceiling and a large
butler's pantry was located to the right.

"Help yourself to anything you'd like."

"Do you cook?" Cleo thought it would be a
waste not to use the kitchen.

"I dabble here and there. Primarily breakfast
stuff. I have a cook, Joan, who makes sure I'm well
fed when I'm in town. Let her know your schedule
and she'll be sure something is prepared for you.
Don't hesitate to let her know if there's anything
you don't like and she'll avoid using those ingredi-
ents."

"I don't think I'll be staying that long."

"Cleo, I think you should stay here for a few
weeks, until it's clear what this creep has in mind.
Make yourself at home."

"Let's take it a day at a time..."

৵

The word she'd use for the next room Drake
had shown her was decadent. Cleo hadn't seen his
bedroom so conceivably there could have been two
rooms in the house that fit that description but
currently she marveled at the home theater. For an
actress, this was her definition of heaven. If she felt
her guest room had been a private oasis then this
room became her biggest indulgence. One side of
the room was filled with extensive shelves of books
and videos. Drake had also shown her an expan-
sive collection of movie and music CDs that were
located in cabinets below the shelves. On the other
side of the room there was a wet bar which includ-

ed a microwave. Between the two walls was a large, cozy sectional couch positioned in front of a built-in theater screen.

Currently Cleo was curled up on the couch with a stadium throw watching Drake as he prepared a bag of microwave popcorn. Her job had been to pick a movie from the list of films Drake had handed her. At first the list had overwhelmed her. There were so many wonderful films to pick from. She couldn't believe he had her favorite movie of all time, *Barefoot in the Park* with Robert Red-Redford and Jane Fonda.

"What would you like to drink?"

"Do you have a Coke?"

"Regular or diet?"

"Regular."

Drake opened a small refrigerator and pulled out two glass bottles containing the famous caramel-colored beverage and set them on the coffee table in front of her. She could hear the muffled sound of the popcorn as it popped in the microwave and the warm smell of melted butter began to fill the room.

How had this happened? How had she ended up on Drake's couch, preparing to snuggle down and watch a movie and eat a bunch of popcorn? This was one of her favorite things to do and she was doing it with Drake in his house.

From the size of the list of movies and the supply of microwave popcorn, it appeared it was one of

Drake's favorite things to do, too. Scary. Cleo was beginning to get comfortable. Too comfortable. And the scary part was she didn't care.

"This should be enough popcorn to get us through the movie." Drake set down a large bowl on the coffee table. "Just let me get a couple of glasses of ice and we'll be ready to start. Did you pick out a movie yet?"

"How does *Barefoot in the Park* sound?"

"Perfect."

It was an enjoyable evening. Although she'd seen the film numerous times before, Cleo always enjoyed seeing it again. She let out a sigh when the ending credits began to roll.

"It ends almost too quickly, doesn't it?" Drake seemed to understand exactly how she felt. She didn't want to let go of Corey and Paul just yet.

"Are you up for another movie?" Drake looked at his watch. "Believe it or not, it's still pretty early."

"Sure, but this time you get to pick."

"Alright, should we stay in the same time frame? How about *What's Up Doc?*"

"I don't think I've ever seen that one."

"It's a wonderful screwball comedy with Ryan O'Neal and Barbra Streisand. I think it would be another perfect movie for this evening."

"Okay, let 'er roll."

Drake picked up the empty popcorn bowl. "Do you want another batch to tide us over for the next film?"

"Sure, I love a popcorn dinner."

"One more batch coming up, unless you'd like to have more of a real meal."

"No. After all the food this afternoon, popcorn is perfect."

The evening was relaxing and cozy. Cleo felt completely safe next to Drake. He was like her knight in shining armor, ready to protect her from the intrusive caller. But she wouldn't be able to stay too long at his house. It was too comfortable, too inviting. And Cleo didn't want to take advantage of his hospitality.

The room was bright when Cleo opened her eyes the next morning. The full picture-windows that had been dark the evening before were bright and clear. Sun sparkled on the ocean surface and Cleo could see a few seagulls circling in the air.

The ocean softly drummed against the shore and had lulled Cleo to sleep. The sound of water was soothing and she felt like burrowing into the covers and never coming out.

Cleo looked at the bedside clock and was surprised that it was still early in the morning. The amount of light had made her believe it was much later in the day. It was a good thing she hadn't overslept. There were too many things she needed to do and there was the last Meyerson audition in the late afternoon. She'd been trying to remain neutral about the audition and quell the rising sense of excitement about the third reading. She did not want her nerves to get the best of her.

Drake had given her a set of house keys the night before and shown her how to use the elaborate alarm system. He was truly a giving and caring man. Her first impression of him being cold and distant had apparently been less accurate than she had thought.

After a quick shower, Cleo walked downstairs to the kitchen. Just a quick slice of toast and she'd be on her way. She could hear the sound of footsteps in the kitchen and she wondered if Drake was up already. He was probably always up early considering the demands of The Stockton Agency.

When Cleo pushed open the swinging door that led into the large kitchen, she was disappointed to see a middle-aged woman bent over an uncooked chicken. Drake was nowhere to be seen.

"Aaah, you must be Cleo." The older woman greeted her as she entered the room. "Drake mentioned you were here and warned me not to be alarmed."

The older woman resembled Julia Childs and Cleo could only guess that this was Joan, the woman Drake had mentioned the night before.

"I'm Joan Harris." The woman confirmed before Cleo had a chance to respond. "I'm preparing a chicken for this evening's meal. Will you be returning to the house in time to eat? Dinner should be served at seven-thirty."

"Yeah, I should be back by then."

"Good. I'm making one of my special recipes. It's a Chinese five-spice chicken stuffed with cilantro and green onion."

"It sounds wonderful."

"If you'd like, I can make you some breakfast. I don't have to have the chicken in the oven for several hours. I was just getting it ready to marinate."

"Actually, I was just going to get some toast and then I was going to head out for the day."

"No problem. Why don't you have a seat over there and I'll make up a quick little continental breakfast for you."

"Oh, that's not necessary."

"Sure it is. Mr. Stockton told me to make sure you were well fed and I intend to keep up my end of the bargain. Do you want coffee or tea?"

Cleo enjoyed watching the other woman work. She herself enjoyed cooking but she rarely had time to prepare anything fancy, particularly since she normally ate alone. It seemed pointless to exert so much energy when there was only one person eating.

Within minutes the older woman was pulling a variety of breads out of the oven, and placing a cup of steaming hot coffee in front of Cleo. The rolls and muffins were warm and a glass of orange juice was freshly squeezed. Cleo normally ate donuts straight out of the box for breakfast, along with a cup of microwaved coffee.

"Where's Dra--, I mean, Mr. Stockton?"

"He's already left for the office. He'll be returning around seven tonight. He mentioned a late
afternoon meeting that would probably detain him
until then."

"Oh."

"Is something wrong?"

"No. Well, yes. Not really. I had been hoping to
catch a ride with him. I don't have any way of getting downtown but I can call a cab."

"Oh, dear, not to worry. Mr. Stockton left the
keys to his car for you to use. He felt it would be
safer than riding a motorcycle considering the circumstances." Joan motioned to a set of keys on the
counter. "I hope you don't mind, but Mr. Stockton
explained a little about your predicament."

"No, I don't mind. Otherwise it would probably
seem odd to have someone suddenly show up out
of the blue and move into the guest room."

"Not to worry, dear. Mr. Stockton is a very nice
man. I wouldn't question anything he did. You
don't find them any better than him, dear."

Cleo finished her breakfast, down to the very
last tasty crumb, before excusing herself to collect
her satchel and organizer. She had reviewed her
schedule the night before. A quick trip to her
apartment to get a few more clothes and then off to
her third interview for the Meyerson film. One advantage of the recent events was that she'd hardly
had a moment to get nervous about her audition.

After heading through to the kitchen to collect
the car keys, Cleo opened the door to the garage.

The black convertible Mercedes Drake had driven the day before was the car that was parked in front of her. Surely she wasn't supposed to drive this car? There must be some kind of mistake. Maybe there was a car parked outside.

"Joan?" Cleo called to the other woman as she re-entered the house. "Which car keys are these?"

"I believe the Mercedes, dear."

"But..."

"Mr. Stockton wasn't sure if you were familiar with a manual transmission so he took the Jeep this morning."

"Okay, just checking." Cleo pulled the garage door shut behind her and looked at the powerful machine in front of her. The thought of driving the car was both frightening and exhilarating. What if something were to happen?

Cleo slid into the driver's seat and examined the dashboard. It resembled the cockpit of a plane. After taking a minute to settle into the unfamiliar seat, she studied the buttons and dials to find the buttons to adjust the two side mirrors. She also adjusted the rear view mirror and checked the brake and made sure the car was in "park" before hesitantly turning the key in the ignition. The car roared to life in the enclosed space of the garage, sounding more powerful than Cleo had expected. Fortunately she remembered to hit the button on the electric garage door opener before putting the car into reverse and backing slowly out of the garage.

It was safe to say it was going to be an interesting day.

CHAPTER EIGHT

The car ended up being very easy to maneuver and it didn't take long for Cleo to feel comfortable behind the wheel. It had been awhile since she'd driven a car and she was enjoying the experience.

She'd been surprised when Raymond had called her to tell her she'd been selected as one of three actresses to read for the final cut on the Meyerson project. Her last reading must have gone better than she'd thought. Actually, her lack of confidence was based more on the woman with the clipboard than anything else. She'd have to be careful today not to have any external distractions.

The ringing of the car phone made Cleo jump in her seat. She wasn't used to all the buttons and contraptions in the car just yet. She'd focused on the mechanics of driving and had ignored the radio, CD changer and phone.

She didn't know if she should answer the phone or not. The call was inevitably for Drake. The only people that knew she had the car were Drake and Joan. Of course the caller could be either one of them trying to reach her.

She decided it was best to leave the phone alone and ask Drake about it later. She didn't mind playing personal secretary while she was driving the car if he wanted.

Cleo pulled the car into the driveway and waved to Mrs. Richards, who gave her a puzzled look.

"My dear, you must have done very well with that commercial to have bought a car like this one."

"Hi, Mrs. Richards. Actually, I'm borrowing it for the day from a friend."

"Nice friend." Mrs. Richards smiled. "It must be fun to be young. That reminds me. A young man was here earlier, looking for you."

Cleo felt a chill pass through her body. "Who was it? Did he talk to you?"

"Well, he asked me if I'd seen you today and I told him I was only your landlady, not your keeper." Cleo smiled. Mrs. Richards was very protective and never revealed any information, no matter how seemingly insignificant.

"Did he tell you his name?"

"No, he just said that he'd catch up with you at the club tomorrow night."

Cleo let out a sigh. It must have been Rock. She could feel the muscles in her back beginning to relax again and she realized how stressful she felt at the thought the mysterious visitor could have been the caller.

"Thanks, Mrs. Richards. I think I know exactly who it was. I'll tell him to leave a name if he bumps into you again."

"No problem. Have a good day, Cleo."

Cleo entered her small apartment and let out a sigh. Although Drake's home was luxurious and she felt completely pampered spending the previous night in his beautiful guest room, this was her home. She resented the caller for disrupting her life the way he had.

Drake had been a perfect gentleman the night before and they had enjoyed lots of popcorn with the two movies. They had snuggled on the couch, laughing together over funny parts in both films. At one point they had laughed so hard they almost spilled the large bowl of popcorn they were sharing.

The first night had gone well. They had talked about the arrangements and they both agreed it was probably best if Cleo planned on spending a week at Drake's home. It would be enough time to assess the situation and they agreed to discuss options at the end of the week. Week by week. Day by day. That was the way Cleo was going to live her life for a while.

With a week in mind, Cleo packed a duffle bag with clothes and a couple of books. She looked around to make sure she had everything she needed before she locked the front door and headed back towards Drake's car.

What was she thinking? She should call her parents and let them know that she would be away for a few days and not to worry. She walked towards the phone and noticed the blinking light on the answering machine for the first time.

She took a deep breath as she pressed the play button. She didn't think the caller would actually leave a message but at this point she didn't know.

Beep. "Hi Cleo, it's Drake. I just spoke to Joan and she told me you were on your way to pick up a couple things at your apartment. Sorry I missed you, but I'll try to reach you on the car phone later."

I guess that means to answer the phone in the car. Cleo laughed. Without speaking to Drake he'd answered her question. Who knows? *Maybe he's psychic without realizing it.*

After a quick call to her mother, she left her apartment and locked the door. It was time for the third and final audition. The butterflies were beginning to swarm.

❧

Drake hung up the phone after leaving a message for Cleo at her apartment. He wished he could shake the uneasy feeling he was having.

The previous evening had been enjoyable. How could he have thought Cleo was like the conniving, selfish Gabriella just reminded him that he couldn't label all actresses the same. During the times they were together Cleo was bright, playful and downright fun to be with. Drake found himself sharing things with her that he'd only told his brother and parents. She was cracking through the thick shell he kept around himself all the time.

While he'd been with Gabriella he'd been afraid to reveal aspects of his personality. He was used to living in a town where personal things were often used to manipulate and destroy people. Gabriella had been one of those types of people although he hadn't known until the end of their relationship. Instinctually he had retained an element of privacy, avoiding complete intimacy.

When he was with Cleo, Drake could see into the depths of her character. She was truly a decent, nice person. He wanted to wrap his arms around her and protect her, take care of her. He didn't want anyone to change her or touch her, especially not the caller. What kind of man made obscene calls?

His feelings of dread were linked to the fact that Drake knew he was beginning to fall in love with Cleo Martin. He dreaded that he wouldn't be able to be with her all the time and take care of her. He dreaded the caller who could disrupt both of their lives. Drake would do anything in his power to stop the caller from harassing Cleo any further.

The buzz of an intercom interrupted Drake's thoughts.

"Mr. Stockton, there's a gentleman on the phone for you. He says his name is, oh my, well...er, "Rock". Do you want the call?"

Drake laughed. "Thanks Rita. Sure, put him through."

❧

The butterflies were finally beginning to fly away, although the audition had ended over an hour earlier. Cleo kept reminding herself that she'd done a good job, that the audition result was out of her hands and that she'd just have to wait. Wait and wait. And the butterflies fluttered. Taking several deep breaths of air to calm her nerves didn't do anything to dispel them.

She had called Raymond as soon as she could find a pay-phone after the audition. She had permission to answer the car phone but didn't feel like incurring charges on a phone that wasn't her own. Raymond was optimistic that they would hear something within a couple days.

The filming was scheduled to start in a month and the search for the ingénue would have to end soon out of necessity. Either way, they would hear something within a week.

Cleo took several minutes to let Raymond know she was spending a week or so at a friend's home and she would get back to him with a number where she could be reached. She also assured him that he could leave messages for her at her apartment. It was critical that an actor's agent know where to contact them at any time.

The rest of the day was her own to enjoy and she savored the ability to drive around town. She had tossed her duffle bag into the trunk of Drake's car and she was reminded of the luxuries a car could provide. She had made due with her motorcycle for a couple of years and had adapted a good system, but Cleo had to be honest with herself; it was a lot easier to haul stuff around. Doing laundry and grocery shopping with a bike as one's only means of transportation was limiting; the most she could handle on her bike was one or two laundry loads and a backpack full of food.

Cleo looked at her watch and decided she had time to do a little shopping. She wanted to look for an appropriate gift for Drake to thank him for his generosity. The only problem was that she didn't have the faintest idea what that should be. From the tour of his home, it appeared Drake Stockton didn't want for much in his life.

As Cleo turned down Beverly Boulevard she hoped she could find the perfect gift in one of the stores and boutiques nearby. Los Angeles was a shopper's paradise. Finding a gift shouldn't be too difficult.

❧

Drake had been surprised when Rita had told him Rock was on the phone. He had enjoyed the afternoon bowling with him and the rest of the gang from Podium but Drake had to admit, he'd spent more time with Cleo than anyone else.

He was glad the younger man had called. It gave him the perfect opportunity to hear Rock's perceptions regarding the caller that was harassing Cleo.

It had concerned Rock that the caller had referred to Cleo by name and cited the commercial.

Drake was reminded of the strong bond between the bouncer and Cleo. It was comforting to know they worked the same shifts and that Rock could help Drake keep an eye on her. He wanted to be with Cleo all the time but Drake knew that was not possible. Rock would be a good second.

The buzz of the intercom reminded Drake that he should try calling Cleo. He wanted to make sure she would be at the house before it got dark. Call him paranoid but he wanted to see what the caller had in mind before venturing out too far. He was still trying to shake a foreboding, nagging feeling.

"Mr. Stockton, Randy from the Carlise Corporation is on the phone. Can you take the call?"

"Sure put him through." Sometimes Drake felt his whole day was spent on the phone.

"Drake! You're a genius. I just saw the first sales figures since the commercial started airing and you're brilliant. Market share has increased by two-percent. Did you hear me? Two-percent! That's almost unheard of. I don't care what you have to do, but I want that girl signed as the regular Heathy Shine Shampoo girl and I want you to film a series of commercials to follow the current one."

Drake smiled. He'd known from the first time he'd seen the commercial in post-production and again with Cleo that it was special. She'd brought a quality to the work that had made the commercial surpass his wildest dreams. He'd even been thinking about submitting it for consideration for a CLIO award.

"I'm glad you like the commercial so much, Randy. I'll make a call and let Cleo know you'd like her to make another commercial. I know she'll be thrilled."

"What's her name?"

"Cleo Martin."

"That's a name to remember, you can bet on it."

"You're right, Randy. I wouldn't bet against you on that in a million years.'

After Drake hung up with Randy, he quickly dialed the Mercedes car phone. After two short rings, Cleo's voice came across the line.

"Having fun?," he asked. Cleo laughed in response.

"You don't know the half of it!"

"I'll take that as an affirmative. I just wanted to check and make sure your day is going alright. Do you think you'll be home for dinner?" Drake liked the way that sounded. *Home.*

"Yup. I finished my audition, stopped by my apartment and now I'm heading towards the beach."

"How did the audition go?" Drake hoped Cleo got the part. Either way, he had some good news to share with her.

"I think it went okay. I won't know for a couple days. My agent is going to call the casting director this afternoon to get an idea about the direction they're heading."

"I'll keep my fingers crossed for you."

"Only your fingers?"

Drake laughed. "Okay, fingers and toes. Cross my heart. Oh, that makes three."

"Good. I need all the help I can get."

"I've got some good news for you. Do you want me to tell you now or during dinner?"

"Oh, tell me now." Cleo voice was excited and bubbly across the phone line.

"No. I think I'll tell you over dinner."

"Drake!"

"Cleo!" Drake answered playfully.

"Hey, I thought that women were terrible teases but men are definitely worse. Are you going to tell me or am I going to have to drive over there and drag it out of you?"

"I guess that depends on your torture technique."

"Believe me, Drake, I can be very persuasive." Cleo's voice had taken on a soft and sexy tone and Drake could feel his body respond to the subtle caress of her words.

"Promises, promises."

"I promise if you tell me now, I'll still torture you later if that's what you want."

"Okay, but kidding aside. I spoke to Randy today and he said the preliminary analysis on the commercial shows a dramatic increase in market share for Healthy Shine."

"That's great news."

"Yeah, it means we both did our job well. But that's not the half of it."

"What could be better than that?"

"Maybe I should have you stop the car before I tell you the rest."

"Drake!"

"I'm serious Cleo, pull over to the side of the road. I don't care what happens to the car but I do care about what happens to you."

Drake could hear the turn signal clicking and he could mentally visualize Cleo turning off the road. Soon her voice replied.

"Okay, I'm safely in a parking space. I've even shut off the engine. I'm ready. What could be better than the commercial going well?"

"Randy wants us to shoot two more commercials to add to the national rotation." Drake could hear Cleo's excited squeal.

"Now I see why you didn't want anything to happen to me!"

"Commercial or not, I still wouldn't want anything to happen to you, Cleo. Don't forget, you promised to torture me later, remember?"

Drake hung up the phone with a big smile on his face. He would say he felt like he was back in high school but he didn't remember having such vivid fantasies when he was younger.

༄

Cleo sat in the car, feeling stunned. A whirlwind of emotions were making her feel dizzy. She was going to shoot two more commercials. Not one, but two! And Drake had been flirting with her.

Everything Cleo could think of to torture Drake with really wasn't very torturous. Actually, what she was thinking of would be downright pleasurable.

What had she been thinking when she'd stopped Drake from kissing her on Mulholland? Realistically she knew she'd stopped him because, at the time, she hadn't really known him. She hadn't fully trusted him yet. Now she felt differently. Very differently. And all she could think of was getting him to kiss her again, and this time not stop.

After a few deep breaths, Cleo felt her hands had stopped shaking enough to drive so she started the powerful engine and pulled back into traffic.

The drive back towards Drake's home was pleasant. The salty sea air grew stronger as she neared the Pacific Ocean and Cleo realized she felt happy. Very happy. She felt safe and secure.

She had been worried the night before after talking to the police about the caller. She had worried that he would take over her life and control her and she didn't like the idea. Although her life had been disrupted and she was living at Drake's home, she couldn't say she really hated her predicament. On a certain level, she almost felt she should thank the harassing caller for bringing her closer to Drake. She wanted to laugh at the irony.

The second parking space in the garage was empty when Cleo pulled the Mercedes to a stop on the left side. Obviously Drake wasn't home yet from the office. Home. There was that feeling again. Cleo would have to be careful not to get caught up in the fantasy. It was too easy to feel like she belonged here. Too easy to feel like she was making a home with Drake.

Joan was in the kitchen when Cleo entered the house shortly after six-thirty. It had taken her longer thank she'd expected to find a gift she felt was perfect for Drake, to thank him for his hospitality. She had the store wrap the fountain pen in plain brown paper with a raffia ribbon and it was safely tucked into a gift bag.

"How was your day, dear?" Joan was scrubbing potatoes at the sink.

"It was wonderful!" Cleo was still excited about the overwhelming events of the day. She had an excessive amount of energy that she didn't know what to do with. "Let me run these things upstairs and I'll be right back down."

Cleo dropped her duffle bag, the gift for Drake and her satchel on the bed as she shrugged out of her jacket. She'd forgotten how warm it was inside the car. She was used to layering her clothes for warmth while she rode her bike.

A few minutes later she re-entered the kitchen and sat down on one of the stools around the butcher's block in the center of the room. "What can I do to help?"

"Oh, that's not necessary, dear. I've got dinner under control. I'm just finishing up these potatoes and the chicken is already in the oven."

"It smells wonderful."

"Why, thank you, dear."

"I can set the table if you'll point me in the direction of the dishes."

"Thank you, but it's already done. If you'd like, you can keep me company."

"Sure, but promise me you'll be sure to let me know if you need any help."

"I promise." The older woman let out a laugh. Cleo was so refreshing and so different than Gabriella. Joan liked her immediately.

The two women enjoyed the next half hour together. Cleo watched in awe as Joan cooked and the older woman didn't hesitate to share cooking tips with her. In turn, Joan asked Cleo what it was like to audition and Cleo relayed some of the funnier escapades she'd had auditioning.

After one story, the two women were laughing so hard, Cleo's ribs hurt and Joan was wiping tears from her eyes. They were still giggling when Drake entered the kitchen.

"Hi, honey, I'm home!" Drake said playfully as he entered. "I'm glad to see you two have gotten to know each other."

"How was your day, Drake?" Cleo was beginning to feel like June Cleaver. Next thing she'd know she'd be helping him with his coat and getting him his slippers.

"My day was great."

Drake picked up a carrot that was on the table in front of him and Joan swatted playfully at his hand. "You're going to ruin your appetite!"

"Not for your cooking, Joan. It's always wonderful." Drake bit into the carrot with a crunch.

Cleo couldn't believe it, but Joan blushed slightly and turned away. Drake didn't seem to notice.

"I have some things to drop off in my study. I'll be down in a few minutes."

"Well, dinner should be ready in about twenty minutes." Cleo marveled at the other woman's efficiency. The potatoes were already sliced and a casserole prepared. It had gone into the oven shortly after Cleo had arrived. The carrots were sliced and were being tossed into a salad with lettuce, tomatoes and cucumber.

"Oh, dear, I forgot to take Mr. Stockton's shirts up to his bedroom. The cleaner delivered them just before you arrived. I'll be right back." Joan dried her hands and started to untie her apron when the timer on the oven started to beep. Joan hesitated.

"I'll take the shirts upstairs and you can get the chicken out of the oven."

"Oh, I couldn't ask you to do that..."

"I don't mind. Really. Where're the shirts?"

"They're on the back of the pantry door. Just hang them in Drake's closet with the other shirts. You can't miss it."

Cleo gathered up the five shirts on the back of the pantry door and started up the stairway that led to the third level of the house. This part of the house had been excluded from the tour the night before and Cleo felt a twinge of curiosity as she neared the top of the flight.

"Drake?" No answer. He was probably in his study. Cleo looked to the left and saw a closed door. To the right was an open door and Cleo could see the corner of a bed. As she walked toward the room, she could see more of the lush furnishings. The carpet was thick under her feet and a bed was to the left of the doorway. It was covered with a blend of plaid and paisley patterns, deep burgundy and hunter green with flecks of cream. The bedroom was similar to her own, with a sitting alcove and view of the Pacific. The window coverings were different. In her room the windows were covered with white, wooden shutters. Drake's windows were hidden by lush, heavy drapes. The room was dark and inviting. Her room was cozy and warm. Drake's was opulent.

As she walked further into the room she saw an armoire and dresser, both constructed of a cherry colored wood. Several pictures were on top of the dresser and Cleo was curious who the variety of people were in the photos.

As she walked over to examine the photographs more closely, she heard the muffled sounds of water coming from the bathroom. Drake! He wasn't in his study, he was in the shower! Cleo wondered what his naked body looked like, glistening with water droplets.

This was dangerous territory. Drake's bedroom, him naked on the other side of the bathroom door and Cleo with an armful of shirts. Better to dump the shirts and run. Cleo felt panic rising inside of her as she searched for the closet entrance. She hoped it wasn't on the other side of the bathroom. Luckily, it was located on the right side of the bedroom, the opposite corner from the bathroom.

She entered the large closet quickly and glanced around fervently, looking for the other shirts. It seemed to take forever to located the crisp cotton shirts and push them to one side, leaving room for the shirts in her hand. Who would have guessed that Drake was such a clothes-horse. Cleo tried to suppress a giggle as she hurried out of the closet.

The giggle caught in her throat as she ran head on into Drake. A damp Drake with only a towel covering his lean, muscled body.

CHAPTER NINE

"Hi, Cleo."

"Hi, Drake." Damn him for being so comfortable. She was a nervous wreck. He was, on the other hand, acting as if he ran into women in his closet all the time. "I was... er, helping Joan..."

"Oh, really?"

"I just brought up some shirts that the cleaner delivered."

"Oh, and here I thought you were here to make good on your promise."

"My promise?"

"I thought maybe you were here to torture me."

Cleo felt a blush as she remembered the thoughts she'd had earlier in the car about the type of torture she had in mind. Drake leaned into the doorway and Cleo tried not to stare at the muscles rippling in front of her. Several droplets of water still glistened on his smooth skin and Cleo drew in her breath. If she thought Drake looked amazing in a suit it was only because she'd never seen him in a towel. This was definitely a good look. Minus the towel promised to be even better.

"Actually, I think you have that the other way around."

"How so?"

"I'd say you're the one torturing me. You're the one wearing only a towel."

Drake looked down at the terry cloth tucked around his hips and started to laugh. "So I am. You think this is torture?"

"Yes...I mean no." Cleo licked her lips nervously. "Minus the towel would be more torturous."

"I think it would depend what happened once the towel was removed. Is that how you're going to torture me? By taking my towel?"

Drake took a step closer and Cleo could smell the faint smell of soap on his skin. She wanted to press against him and see if he felt as good as he smelled. Before she realized what she was doing she reached her hand out and smoothed the water droplets on the surface of Drake's skin, massaging them dry.

Drake let out a groan. "Cleo, you're making it very hard to keep my promise to you."

"What promise?"

"The promise to be just friends."

"Oh, that promise." Cleo pressed her lips against the nape of Drake's neck and he let out another groan. She kissed him again and then looked him directly in the eyes. "I give you permission to break that promise, Drake."

He pulled her against his chest and kissed her firmly. Her hands were pressed against his chest and Cleo could feel the strong beating of Drake's heart as he kissed her. She moved her hands up his chest and wound them around the back of his neck, intertwining her fingers with his hair. Drake deepened their kiss and Cleo could feel his body hardening under the towel. She was conscious of her own clothes and suddenly felt overdressed. Drake must have been thinking the same thing because he was slipping his hands under her blouse and finding the clasp to her bra. As he took one of her breasts firmly in his hand, she let out a moan. She wanted to be closer to him. She pushed her hips forward, feeling the throbbing of his erection press against her.

Drake leaned forward and wrapped his arm around the small of Cleo's back and lifted her feet off the floor and began to carry her towards the bed. She sunk into the luxurious covers as he gently lowered her onto the bed. She pulled at her shirt, lifting it over her head and slipped out of her lace bra. Drake reached for the closure of her jeans and together they quickly removed the clothes that were suddenly feeling bulky and heavy. Drake put his hands on her hips and slowly slid her lace panties down the length of her legs.

Drake was standing at the edge of the bed, looking down at her with an expression of wonderment. "Cleo, you are so beautiful. Are you sure you're ready to do this?"

She caught his hand in her own and guided it between her legs. As he gently stroked her, Cleo arched her back. She wanted to feel him inside her. The ache was growing stronger with each circular motion of his hand. She reached over and pulled at the towel, removing the last barrier between them. His body was perfect.

She took both of his hands in her own and pulled him down on top of her. She could feel his body wrap around her, strong and warm. She reached out and took him into her hand and moved gently but firmly up and down the length of his erection. She could feel him getting firmer as she guided him between her legs and urged him closer.

"Just a second, honey." Drake reached for the drawer of the bedside table and groped for a condom. Cleo writhed on the bed in anticipation as she watched him tear open the foil packet. Together they slid on the latex shield and Drake thrust inside her, pulled back and thrust again. He fit perfectly.

Making love to Drake Stockton was definitely better than the fantasy. Cleo ran her fingers down his back, settling them on his backside, urging him deeper. Her legs wrapped around him. She didn't want him to do anything differently as she felt a wave of climax wash over her. Her breath caught in her throat as she climaxed again. This had never happened to her before.

They both froze as Joan's voice echoed from the lower level.

"Mr. Stockton?"

"Yes, Joan?" Cleo was amazed that his voice sounded clear and calm. Well, almost.

"Dinner's on the table. I'll see you in the morning unless there's something else you'd like me to do this evening."

Drake smiled. "No that's fine, Joan. Thank you. Have a safe drive home."

"Goodnight."

"'Night."

When they were sure the older woman had moved away from the bottom of the stairs, Cleo started to giggle.

"I forgot to tell you. Dinner's ready."

"The nice thing about chicken -- it's good hot or cold. I hope you don't mind but we're going to eat later. I'm not finished with the appetizer yet."

"Good, because neither am I."

They spent their evening making love, feeding each other dinner in front of the fireplace and making love again in front of the glowing embers. Afterwards they lay intertwined, watching the final flickers of the fire.

"Cleo?"

"Hmmm?"

"I like your style of torture. Anytime you want to do it again, go ahead."

"You sound like Br'er Rabbit."

"What do you mean?"

"Br'er Rabbit told the fox that he could do anything but throw him in the briar patch as if that would be the worst torture in the world. In reality it was his haven. I think I'm going to call you Br'er Rabbit from now on."

"Well, I think Cleo suits you just fine. Drake stood up and leaned down to pull Cleo up into his arms and started to walk upstairs. "Time to go to bed."

"Drake! I can walk on my own, you know."

"Yes, I know you can. I just want to make sure you end up in the right bed this evening. Mine."

"Well, Drake, by definition, they're both yours if you think about it." Cleo teased playfully.

"Yes, but yours is a queen size and mine is a king. We're going to want the extra room with what I've got planned."

Cleo blushed as she thought about the possibilities. "Lead on, King Br'er."

Drake laughed as he shut the bedroom door.

૨૭

Cleo stretched happily, like a cat. She would have been purring if she'd been able. She was curled up in bed with the sunlight shining in the window.

Drake had left recently for his office and Cleo was enjoying a few minutes of the sunny morning before starting her own day. Last night had been incredible but Cleo reminded herself that this was only a temporary fantasy. After the week was over she would be moving back to her apartment and the physical relationship she was sharing with Drake would inevitably come to an end.

He'd said nothing about the physical change in their relationship and Cleo wasn't ready to vocalize the ultimate end to what they were experiencing. She would just have to keep her emotions in check and be prepared to move out in a week's time. She tried not to listen to the little voice inside of her that warned her that her emotions were already involved and that she was playing a dangerous game with Drake Stockton.

Cleo had to admit that men and women viewed sex differently. Men seemed able to be physical without any emotional attachment. Cleo was realizing how different she was. Her inner voice kept invading her feelings of bliss and to avoid it, Cleo walked into the bathroom and turned on the shower.

"Good morning, Joan." Cleo greeted the older woman half an hour later, feeling energetic and revitalized after a brisk shower.

"Good morning, Ms. Martin."

"Joan, please call me Cleo. When you call me Ms. Martin I feel like my mother is standing right behind me."

The older woman laughed. "Okay. Good morning, Cleo. What would you like for breakfast?"

Yup. This was a fantasy life that was going to come to an end in a week. Actually, less than a week. Five days.

"Toast and coffee would be great."

Within minutes, Joan was placing a plate of buttered toast in front of her, along with a steaming mug of cinnamon-laced coffee. It was wonderful.

"Will you be here for dinner?"

"I'm planning on it." Cleo remembered the feast from the night before. Even with the delay it had been superb. "Last night's dinner was one of the best meals I think I've ever had." Joan smiled and glanced down at her hands. "Thank you." Her modesty surprised Cleo. Surely she knew her talents in the kitchen.

"May I get a sneak peek of the menu for tonight?"

"Certainly. If there's anything you don't like, let me know." Cleo listened as Joan outlined a variety of dishes, each one sounding more delectable than the first.

"You'll hear no complaints from me. Everything sounds wonderful."

The sound of the telephone interrupted their conversation. Joan answered after the second ring and after a few words, passed the phone towards Cleo.

She felt her heart in her throat as she took the extended receiver. Raymond had promised to call as soon as he heard about the Meyerson casting.

"Hello?" Her heart skipped a beat as she recognized Drake's voice on the other end of the line.

"How'd you like to have lunch today?"

"Let me check my calendar, but I think that would work."

Drake laughed. "If you could, pencil me in."

Cleo opened her organizer and scanned the entries for the day. "I've got an audition at eleven-thirty. If you don't mind waiting until one, I think I can make it."

"I can wait. I'll see you then."

"Where do you want to meet?"

"Aaah, that's a good question. Why don't you come to my office after your audition and we'll go from here."

"Okay, I'll see you there around one, give or take."

"I'll be here." Drake paused. "Hey, Cleo?"

"Yeah?"

"Last night was incredible."

Cleo hoped Joan didn't see the deep blush that darkened her cheeks. "I had a good time, too, Drake."

❧

The audition went well and Cleo made it to Drake's office just past one o'clock. She was surprised the guard recognized her and greeted her with a cheerful welcome.

"Hello, Ms. Martin. Mr. Stockton is expecting you. If you'll follow me, I'll get you on the express elevator." They walked together and the guard talked excitedly beside her.

"My wife just loves the commercial you did. She went out and bought the shampoo as soon as she saw it. She's going to die when she hears that I actually met you today."

Cleo was at a loss for words. Admiration from strangers was new ground to cover. "Thank you..." Cleo glanced at the guard's name badge. "Bob."

They stopped in front of the ornate doors of Drake's private elevator. Bob entered a code and the doors opened.

"Tell your wife I think she'll love the shampoo. I've been using it for a while and I think it's great."

"I'll do that, Ma'am."

"Call me Cleo, please."

Bob grinned. "Sure, Cleo."

The ride up in the elevator was smooth and quick. Who would have guessed that she would be here, involved with the owner of The Stockton Agency. Don't get caught up in the fantasy, Cleo. This is sure to end when you move out of his house.

Cleo stepped off the elevator and was greeted by Drake's secretary.

"Ms. Martin. If you'll come this way, Mr. Stockton is expecting you."

"Thank you, Rita."

"Before you go in, let me tell you how much I enjoy your commercial. I feel re-energized every time it comes on TV."

"Thank you." Cleo smiled as she pushed open the door to Drake's office. The compliments from Drake's staff should be expected. It would seem likely that they would be apprised of the current advertising the company generated.

Drake was on the phone as she entered the office and he waved her inside.

"Yes, Randy. We're in pre-production right now. If you're interested in attending the filming, I'll make sure you have the schedule. Charlie is in charge of the production. You can call either one of us for details."

Drake held up two fingers to indicate he would be off the phone shortly. "Did you sign-off on the art boards and concept yet? Good. I'll check with Charlie and we'll be in touch with the final production schedule."

Drake replaced the receiver and looked at Cleo. "We need to talk about the production phases for the two commercials. Do you have your schedule with you?"

Cleo pulled out her organizer and Drake continued. "Block off the week after next, along with the week after that. When I know more specifics, I'll let you know."

"Okay." Cleo was disappointed. She realized she thought it was going to be a personal, intimate lunch with Drake. Apparently it was going to be a working session.

Drake stood up and walked around his desk. "Okay, I'm now officially on lunch. No more work until we get back. Deal?"

Cleo laughed, relieved that her initial thoughts had been accurate. "Deal."

"There's a great little bistro around the corner. Does that sound good?"

"It sounds great." Cleo stood up, preparing to leave with Drake.

"Before we leave, I want to greet you properly." Drake smiled. "The way I would have greeted you if I hadn't been on the phone." Drake pulled her into his arms and kissed her thoroughly. Cleo could feel herself melting into his chest as she kissed him back. Drake certainly was full of surprises. Her legs felt shaky as he released her. This man was certainly dangerous considering the way she reacted to him.

Drake smiled as he let her go. "I've been thinking of doing that all morning." Cleo giggled as she acknowledged to herself that she'd spent a good portion of the morning entertaining similar thoughts.

"Oh, you think that's funny, do you?" Drake was laughing as well.

"No. It's just...well let's just say that great minds think alike."

"I like your style, Cleo. Let's get out of here before I feel a need to barricade the door and finish the rest of my morning fantasy."

"Only if you promise to share the rest of it with me tonight."

"You can count on it."

The bistro was quaint and charming and oddly placed in Westwood Village which catered more to trendy and chain restaurants.

They laughed together as Cleo recounted the audition from the morning. She had fun telling Drake about her impressions of the audition and the stresses of reading with a person that wasn't a fellow actor.

"That reminds me, Drake. I have to pick up sides from Raymond this afternoon. Do you think you'll be able to run lines with me tonight?"

"What do I have to do?"

"Just read the lines that aren't my part."

"Sure, that sounds like fun."

"You never know, Drake, you might be an actor and not know it."

Drake laughed. "I don't anticipate any career changes in the near future."

"My grandmother told me a person can do anything they want to do, so don't discount acting so quickly."

"Your grandmother never saw me in my grade-school play. As I recall, the teacher was out on stress leave shortly after the production."

"You're kidding!"

"Yeah, but I was still bad. Really, really bad."

"I'm sure you weren't as awful as you think."

"Believe me, I was so bad my parents kept reminding me of all the things I excelled at to try to make me feel better."

"Your parents sound like good people."

"They are. Your grandmother sounds like she was quite a lady as well." Drake looked serious for a minute. "Do you ever take off the bracelet she gave you?"

"Why do you ask?"

"Because I noticed you wore it all last night and even slept with it on."

"No, I don't take it off, even when I shower. Does that bother you?"

"Not at all. But aren't you worried about losing it?"

"Nope. I had a jeweler add a safety chain so even if the clasp comes loose, it won't fall off my wrist. I wear it all the time as a constant reminder that I can do anything I want to do. Even when an audition goes badly I can look down at the bracelet and be reminded that something eventually will work out. My grandmother was always very optimistic about life."

"She sounds like an incredible lady."

"I wish you could have met her. She died several years ago."

"Hearing you speak about her, I feel like I know her. At least on a certain level."

"I find it comforting to know in many ways she lives on in my memories."

The waiter placed their check on the table and Cleo realized that the meal had gone by quickly. She didn't want the time with Drake to end. Without wanting to, she acknowledged the growing feelings she had for him. Whether she liked it or not, she would be moving out of his house in five days. That was the reality of the situation.

Cleo looked at her watch. "I've got to get to Raymond's office. I also have to pick up some things at my apartment but I should be back to your house by five."

"I don't like you going to your apartment by yourself. Do you mind waiting until this evening so we can go over together?"

Cleo secretly acknowledged her own fears about going alone to her apartment and she was relieved he offered to go with her.

"Sure, we can go tonight."

She didn't want Drake to know of her insecurities. He'd already been so generous. Besides, she couldn't hide forever. Sooner or later she would have to return to her old life and her apartment, alone.

"I should be home by seven."

ॐ

"Cleo, darling, come on in." Raymond was a flurry of energy. He was a middle-aged, slender man with blonde hair that hid the gray that was beginning to filter throughout. He approached life as if he had just consumed twelve cups of coffee.

"I've been trading calls all day with the Meyerson people."

"Any word yet?"

"Well, I did hear that they eliminated one of the other girls so it's down to you and one other person."

Cleo felt nervous happiness flare inside her. She wasn't out of the woods yet, but she was close. Very, very close.

"I don't want to discourage you, but they may require one more reading. They sent the reels to Meyerson directly and his style has always been to cast based on the recorded film. But he may make an exception and have you come back in one more time."

Cleo listened patiently while Raymond continued. "His belief is that film doesn't lie and readings that are done live may create a bias. One more reading is unlikely but a possibility."

"That's an unusual way to cast a film, isn't it? Especially considering how much money is involved."

"That's what I love about you, Cleo. You understand the business elements of making a film. So many people don't understand this is a business like any other. Money talks."

"It just seems odd that Meyerson would decide final casting based on the video recordings of the readings."

"Darling, Meyerson's a true eccentric but he's one of the elite. Certainly a feather in your cap if you get the part. Three months of temperamental hell from a director really isn't all that bad. Trust me. If you get this part, you'll float through the entire project."

Cleo knew Raymond was right. The Meyerson project promised to be fun and unique. Besides, she'd heard Meyerson was a stickler for accuracy but fair when dealing with actors.

Raymond tossed pages across his desk towards Cleo. "These are for the latest audition."

Cleo had to admire Raymond. He was a good agent. She didn't know how many auditions she'd been on during the last month. Most of being successful was insuring that you were seen by the people who made casting decisions. Unfortunately talent was only a small part of the equation. "What are these sides for?"

Raymond filled her on the audition details for the next half hour. As he walked her towards his office door he put his arm around her in a paternal, soothing way. "Keep your chin up. I have a good feeling about the Meyerson project. And even if it doesn't work out, a lot of other things are in the works."

"I'm not worried, Raymond.'

"Good girl. That reminds me; I got a call from The Stockton Agency. Congratulations on the additional commercials. The contracts should be here by the end of the week."

"Have you seen the first one yet?"

"Are you kidding? I think I've seen it at least ten times. Every time I turn on the television it's on."

Cleo smiled. She didn't watch enough television to know how often it came on. Drake had given her a schedule of the air dates but she had only glanced at the pages. It was hard to imagine that the commercial was being played as often as it was and it was hard to make the schedule take a concrete form from the vague numbers on the page.

"I'll call you after the audition tomorrow," she said as she picked up her satchel and started toward the door.

"I'm sure I'll hear something about the Meyerson film soon. I'll call you as soon as I hear anything."

Cleo leaned over Raymond's desk and scribbled Drake's home number on a pad of paper. "Remember, I'm staying at a friend's house this week. Here's his number."

"His? Sounds intriguing." Raymond winked as he took the sheet of paper. "I'll only call if I need too."

"Raymond! Call if you want too."

"Don't worry, I will." Raymond was still smiling as she walked out the door.

❧

Dinner was as wonderful as Cleo anticipated and she felt like she could melt into the seat of the car as they drove towards her apartment. She'd eaten too much food and now she felt drowsy.

She watched Drake as he drove. She felt comfortable just sitting next to him. Dinner with him had been fun. Every time they got together, time

seemed to fly by without her noticing. She was getting way too comfortable.

Cleo tried to sit up in her seat and shake away
the sleep that was threatening to overcome her.
"I'm not being very good company, am I?"

"That's okay. Go ahead and sleep if you want.
I'll wake you when we get there."

Cleo tried to keep her eyes open but they felt
heavier and heavier and everything faded to black.
She started to slip into a dream state as Drake
pulled the car into her driveway. As she tried to
shake away the sleepiness she struggled between
her hazy dream state and reality. She was disappointed they were arriving at the time they did. The
dream had included Drake.

"Cleo?"

"Hmmm?"

"We're here, honey." Drake was stroking her
arm, encouraging her to wake up.

Cleo turned in her seat and faced Drake. "I was
just dreaming about you."

"I hope it had a lot of torture in it."

"I don't know, I woke up before I was able to
dream too much."

"I can help you finish it if you'd like." Drake
kissed her softly on the mouth.

"Sure, the real thing is always better than a
dream anyway."

Cleo pulled Drake towards her. The problem
was she liked having Drake near her, touching her.
She found herself doing things she normally didn't

do. She was much more aggressive than she'd been with any man before.

She'd been fearless the night before. Drake wrapped in a towel was certainly a sight to cause even the strongest of women to go weak in the knees. She'd acted without thinking He seemed a very willing participant, then and now.

"You know, I have a bed inside my apartment that might be a little more comfortable. Bucket seats with a stick shift in between aren't the most desirable of locations." Cleo suggested.

"I don't know... I kind of like feeling like I'm back in high school, making out at a drive-in movie."

"I'll pop a movie into the VCR and we can pretend."

"Let's go." They quickly got out of the car and Cleo fumbled for her keys. "You really do make me feel like I'm back in high school. The only difference is that my father isn't on the other side of the door waiting for me to return from a date. I don't think I was kissed until I was eighteen. The shadow of my father in the window scared away all my dates."

Drake pulled Cleo into his arms and kissed her thoroughly. "I like your father more and more."

Somehow they managed to open the door and get inside Cleo's apartment. Drake kicked the door shut behind them and they moved together, kissing as they went, depositing clothes on the floor as they made their way to the bed.

Cleo was wearing a lace bra and panties and Drake was stripped down to his briefs when the phone rang.

"Whoever's calling has great timing." Drake continued to kiss Cleo as he reached for the clasp of her bra.

Cleo pulled back as the phone continued to ring. "It might be Raymond about the casting."

"And it might not be."

"Do you mind. I won't be long, I promise." Cleo kissed him before walking over to the table and picking up the phone.

The voice on the other end of the line was familiar. Too familiar. "Where have you been, I've been trying to call you. And, who is that man you're with?"

CHAPTER TEN

"Who is this?" Cleo asked as she pressed the record button on her answering machine. The tape began to record their conversation.

"Aaah, come on Cleo... You know who I am. We're destined to be lovers. I knew as soon as I saw your commercial we were going to end up together."

"You're wrong. I don't even know who you are."

"Sure you do, baby. It was love at first sight, for both of us. I can hardly wait to feel you wrapped around me. I've been a patient man until now, but soon, baby, soon we can be together."

Cleo felt sick. A wave of nausea washed over her and she fought the urge to slam down the phone. The voice sounded familiar but she wasn't sure if it was from the calls or an actual encounter with the caller. She searched her memory, hoping to make some connection with the caller and someone from her past. Her mind was coming up with a big, fat zero.

"Cleo, I've got to go now, but I'll see you soon... You can count on it."

Drake was behind Cleo, wrapping his arms around her, comforting her. "Was it that creep again?" Cleo nodded. "What did he say to you? You're shaking like a leaf."

Cleo reached over the answering machine and pressed the play button. The lurid voice of the caller filled the room and Drake pulled Cleo closer.

"If I ever get my hands on that guy he's going to end up in the hospital."

"Drake, I'm scared. He's watching me. He's watching us. What am I going to do?"

"Come on, let's get your things together and we'll head back to the house. We'll call Deputy Schmidt and see if they were able to trace the call." Drake reached over to the answering machine and pulled out the tape. "Quick thinking to record the conversation. We're going to put a stop to this one way or another."

Cleo started to gather up her clothes from the floor. Drake dressed while she looked for the books that she needed. She also collected additional clothes. She didn't feel comfortable coming to her home anymore and she wanted to ensure she had everything she needed for a while.

"Ready?" Cleo nodded. She felt numb from the recent events. She felt she was riding an emotional roller coaster.

They drove in silence towards Drake's home. Drake looked dark and brooding when Cleo looked at him and she could see his jaw was set in determination. She reached over and touched his thigh with her hand. "It's going to be okay, isn't it?"

Drake closed his hand over hers and squeezed gently. "It will be."

He maneuvered the car into the garage and shut off the engine. "Why don't we make a fire and relax in front of the fireplace."

"That sounds perfect."

"I don't think there's much we can do tonight and tomorrow I'm going to look into getting a private investigator."

"Drake, I can't afford to hire an investigator. The phone trace should be working within a few days." Cleo hated the idea of being so disrupted from her life and she was feeling like her options were being limited one by one. "I think I'm going to start looking for a new apartment."

"Let's sleep on it and discuss our options in the morning."

Drake had a fire started within a few minutes and they curled up together and looked at the flickering flames. Cleo was thankful that Drake was a part of her life. She leaned into his chest and felt protected.

The phone rang and Cleo felt herself stiffen. Was she going to react to the phone like this every time it rang in the future? She felt like one of Pavlov's dogs with an automatic reaction to the sound of a bell.

Drake didn't move. "The machine will pick it up. I think we've had enough phone calls for the evening."

The answering machine clicked on and Drake's voice urged a caller to leave a message. Beep.

"Hi, this is Raymond. I was given this number for Cleo Martin..."

Cleo was on her feet quickly. "My god, Drake, he must have heard something about the Meyerson film."

Drake laughed. "I guess maybe we should answer it, then." He was on his feet, reaching for the phone and handing it towards Cleo.

"Hello, Raymond?"

"Honey. You didn't tell me your friend was Drake Stockton. My, my, darling, you'll have to tell me about this sometime over a cup of coffee."

"Don't count on it Raymond."

"I've been trying to reach you for a while. Finally decided to leave a message."

"We were out on an errand."

"Cleo, honey, I heard from the Meyerson casting group."

She tried to shake the feeling of dread that was rising in her throat.

"I'm sorry, honey, but they went with the other actress. If it makes you feel any better they said it was close. Really, really close."

"Oh. Okay. Thanks for calling, Raymond."

"Honey, there will be other parts. You're about to break through. I can feel it."

Cleo hung up the phone and looked at Drake.

"Well?"

"I didn't get the part." She tried to mask her disappointment.

"I'm sorry, Cleo. I know how important it was to you." He wrapped his arms around her.

"It's okay." Cleo felt the last bit of energy drain from her body. She just wanted to curl up in a ball and sleep for several days.

"I know it doesn't seem like it now, but everything is going to be okay."

"That's what Raymond said."

"Smart man."

"Today has certainly been one of the worst in my life."

"Come on, let's go to bed. Tomorrow is bound to be better."

Cleo tried to smile. "I don't think it could get any worse." Her life certainly had had some dramatic ups and downs lately. "Well, I've got the audition tomorrow and we start shooting the other two commercials soon."

"Cleo, it's okay to mourn the loss of this part."

"What do you mean?"

"I mean it's alright to be disappointed. Just remember that tomorrow always brings something new. Something that promises to be better. I'm sure you're going to be great at the audition tomorrow."

Cleo had to laugh. "Were you a psych major in college?"

"No, Business and Economics. But I learned that if you try hard enough at something you will eventually succeed."

"Thanks, Drake." Cleo stood on her toes and kissed him on the cheek.

"For what?"

"For understanding."

🐚

The audition had gone well but Cleo couldn't shake the apprehensive feeling that crept upon her. She felt like she was being watched. Watched as she drove to the interview. Watched as she exited the studio. She rationalized that it was probably a common response, considering the recent events. The caller had been very clear about his intentions to confront her.

Cleo unlocked the door to the Mercedes and climbed inside. Drake had given her his private number at the agency and she dialed the number quickly. He had been so concerned about her leaving the house alone she wanted to assure him everything was alright. Although the tingling down her spine made her feel differently.

Cleo looked around the busy street as she listened to the phone ring. What could go wrong? It was daylight and lots of people were around, busy with the events of their day.

What would the caller do? Try to attack her in the street in broad daylight with a group of people around? Not likely. Cleo tried to look for the humor in the situation to shake her feelings of dread.

"Hi, Drake." She loved hearing his deep voice on the other end of the phone.

"Cleo! Are you alright?"

"Yeah, I'm fine. I keep looking over my shoulder but no one's there."

"How did the audition go?"

"The usual...'Thank you for coming in... very nice... we'll be in touch with Raymond.'" Cleo mimicked the casting person's diction perfectly.

"What are your plans for the rest of the day?"

"I'm going to grab a sandwich for lunch and then head back to the house."

"Why don't you have Joan make something for you when you get there?"

"Because I'm hungry now and I refuse to let this man disrupt my life any more than he already has. If I want to get a sandwich, I'm going to get a sandwich."

"Okay, okay. I was just asking."

"I know. I'm sorry. I guess this guy's made me a little cranky."

"Understandably. I'm going to try to get out of the office by five tonight."

"It would be nice to see you for a little bit before I go to Podium."

"Do you have to dance tonight? I worry about you being there with this creep on the loose."

"I feel like a broken record but I don't want my life disrupted any more than it has been."

"I know, I know. I was just asking."

"Don't worry, Rock will be there. If it makes you feel any better you can drop me off and pick me up."

"Sounds like a good plan. So where are you now and where are you eating?"

"You're beginning to sound like my father," Cleo laughed. As she continued she tried to sound like a local tour guide. "I will be dining at Nate & Al's, a wonderful local establishment that serves some of the best sandwiches in town, followed by a lovely coastal drive along the blue waters of the Pacific Ocean. The total tour should take approximately an hour or so. Once arriving at the beach house I plan on taking a nap to ensure that I am well rested and ready to dance this evening at the posh and exclusive nightclub, Podium."

Drake was laughing by the time she finished. "Humor me. Call me when you're done eating."

"Alright. I'll call you as I'm enjoying the coastal blue waters of the Pacific."

"I'll be here."

Cleo smiled as she hung up the phone and started the car. She slipped easily into traffic and headed for the famous deli in Beverly Hills. She didn't notice the dark sedan that pulled into traffic several cars behind her.

❧

Drake hung up the phone after talking to Cleo. He wished he could shake the uneasy feeling he had. Cleo was right – he was acting like her father.

He pressed the button on the intercom and waited for his secretary to respond. "Rita, will you clear my calendar for the afternoon. I have to go out unexpectedly."

"Sure, Mr. Stockton. What should I tell Mr. Wilson? He just arrived for your lunch appointment."

Drake had forgotten the luncheon with the

young man. "Don't tell him anything."

"Yes, sir."

"Actually, Rita, please send him in."

The door to Drake's office opened and a young man wearing a business suit entered the room. His large frame filled the entrance. Drake almost didn't recognize him in a suit and tie.

"How do sandwiches from Nate & Al's sound?"

"Great, let's go."

After Drake collected his jacket and car keys, the two men walked to the door.

"Your secretary said you were called out of the office unexpectedly this afternoon. Would it be better to reschedule our lunch?"

Drake smiled. "Actually, Rock, today couldn't be better. I'll tell you about it on the way."

They rode the elevator down to the parking garage. Drake walked towards a dark green Jeep and Rock followed. He quickly unlocked the doors and the two men started on their way.

It didn't take long for Drake to fill Rock in on the recent events.

"Man, I thought that creep had given up."

"Now it seems he wants to get to know Cleo a little better. That's what makes me nervous."

"Sounds like a loose cannon with a few missing screws."

"Something's a little loose, that's for sure."

"Man, Cleo's one helluva woman. She doesn't deserve to be harassed like this. No one does."

"I can't shake the bad feeling I have today. I know she's not going to like us charging into Nate & Al's but I'll feel more comfortable knowing she's alright."

"Hey, don't worry. If everything's alright we just

tell her a couple of friends thought it would be fun to join her for lunch. No harm in that."

Drake laughed. "Yeah, but I know Cleo well enough to know she likes her independence. She doesn't like anyone telling her what to do."

Rock looked serious. "You're right, but I also know her well enough to know that she'll appreciate the thought."

"I hope so. Just as long as she doesn't think my testosterone is overreacting."

Now it was Rock's turn to laugh. "No problem -- we'll just tell her it was mine."

Normally the drive from Westwood to Beverly Hills was only a few minutes but Drake's nerves made him feel like the trek was taking forever. The lunch hour crowd wasn't helping the traffic congestion and Drake gripped the steering wheel in frustration.

"Why do I feel like every minute counts?"

"Little or no sleep and an overactive imagination?"

"You're probably right. I didn't get much sleep last night."

Drake thought about the night before. The voice on the tape had played over and over in his mind. He had admired Cleo's ability to slip into slumber considering the day's events. He had watched her sleep, trying to figure out a way to keep her safe without impacting her freedom. No solution had come readily to mind and his apprehension flared.

As Drake pulled into the public parking lot that paralleled the delicatessen, he saw the Mercedes. Cleo was still here and everything appeared to be normal. He let out the breath he was holding and began to relax.

Drake rolled down his window and took the parking ticket from an attendant who instructed him to park anywhere in the lot. He eased the Jeep into a spot near the Mercedes and he and Rock walked towards the restaurant.

❧

Cleo had enjoyed a thick pastrami sandwich on rye with coleslaw. She'd used the last half hour to relax, enjoy her food and focus on her goals and objectives.

She always found it beneficial to plan the future when something didn't work out in the recent past. So she hadn't gotten the Meyerson film. She knew there would be other opportunities. She wrote her goals out one by one.

The exercise included writing down anything and everything that she wanted to do with her life. Some of the items were things she knew she would never do -- like climbing Mt. Everest -- but she put them down anyway. The final step was to number the activities to place an importance or priority for each and then pursue and conquer.

In the past when Cleo had written out her list, acting was always the number one goal. Now she wasn't so sure. Damn Drake for sneaking into her life the way he had. Relationships and family had moved up more than several notches on her list of priorities. She was having trouble picking one over the other. The problem was she wanted her cake and to eat it, too.

As soon as she found another apartment she would be moving out of Drake's home. She would have to find something quickly. It was going to hurt too much if she delayed the inevitable. Drake had only offered his home on a temporary basis.

Cleo felt sad knowing, in reality, that everything had changed for her. How could men be so different when it came to sex, love and relationships? Nothing had changed for Drake. His world had remained the same.

Cleo let out a sigh as she paid for her lunch. She was tired. The previous evening had drained her of her energy. Better to drive back to the house and nap in preparation for the evening ahead.

She started to walk towards the Mercedes. As she went, she sifted through the contents of her satchel, looking for the car keys. She wasn't used to having so many keys and had tossed them into her large bag so she wouldn't lose them. The irony was that she'd succeeded in losing them in her bag instead. Makeup, change and papers came readily to hand and she finally stopped, focusing all her attention on finding the keys.

She didn't notice the footsteps until the rhythm of her own was removed. The footsteps that sounded behind her stopped abruptly. As silence engulfed her, Cleo felt panic rising in her throat. Why would the footsteps stop so suddenly unless it was someone following behind her.

She turned to confront the person behind her and let out a sigh of relief when she saw who it was. "Oh, 'hi.' You scared me for a second. I thought someone was trying to sneak up on me. How are you, Larry?"

Their blind date hadn't been memorable and she was surprised to find she even remembered his name as she looked at him. After their initial date, she'd asked Ju-Dee why she'd thought they would be a good match and the other woman embarrassingly admitted that he'd seen Cleo at Podium and had pressured her into making the match.

Larry stood in front of her.

"Hi Cleo."

She felt a chill run up her spine. His voice was different in person than it was on the phone and yet it was clearly the same voice as the menacing one she'd been hearing for weeks.

"I told you we'd be together soon. I was just waiting for you to be alone."

Cleo's mind was racing as she tried to figure out how to get away from him. She had no idea what would trigger this man. Their date had been uninteresting. He had been nervous and self-conscious throughout the evening. Now he seemed disturbed and was clearly delusional.

"I told you it was love at first sight for both of us. I waited for you to call after our date and the phone never rang. For weeks I waited. I knew something was wrong. Then it occurred to me that you must have lost my number and been desperately trying to get in touch with me."

"No, Larry." Cleo looked around, trying to find a way out of the situation. The man in front of her was strong enough to over-power her. She felt confident that he wouldn't get aggressive during the day with other people on the street.

He didn't notice her interruption. "My number isn't listed so I knew you had no way of getting in touch with me..."

"Larry, I don't even know your last name. How would I have been able to call information?"

"See? I knew there was a reason you hadn't called. I figured it was that guy who's been bothering you and getting in the way of us being together. He was preventing you from calling, keeping you trapped at his home."

"No, Larry, it hasn't been like that at all." She tried to assess the reaction of the man in front of her.

"It doesn't matter now. Now we can be together without him getting in the way." Larry grabbed her arm roughly and pulled her towards an alleyway away from restaurant. The Mercedes was located in the parking lot on the other side of the building.

"Larry, I can't go with you right now. I need to go to my car to use the phone." He looked suspicious of her request.

"I don't live far from here. You can use the phone at my house and then we can make love."

Cleo felt panic rising in her voice and mentally told herself to speak calmly.

"But I have an appointment I have to cancel if I'm going to go off with you. You understand don't you?" Her voice shook a little and she hoped he hadn't notice. If she could make it to the Mercedes, she would be alright.

"Well..."

Cleo turned towards the parking lot and started towards the car. She couldn't believe what she saw. She blinked twice as Drake and Rock came around the corner, coming towards her.

"Drake!...Rock! I'm over here."

Rage flared as Larry gripped her arm tighter. "He's no good for you. I won't let him come between us."

Cleo stumbled and almost fell as Larry yanked her forward. "I'm going to kill that guy." The words paralyzed Cleo. This man could do anything to her as long as Drake wasn't hurt.

"Larry, everything's going to be alright. You said you lived near here." She tried to distract him and divert his attention away from the two approaching men.

"Let's go." Larry continued to yank her by the arm and pulled her into the alley. As they rounded the turn, Cleo saw the last glimpse of Drake and Rock as they ran towards her. Speed was going to be critical. As long as Larry didn't make any turns before Drake and Rock had a chance to make it around the corner. She stumbled, trying to slow the crazed man at her side but he continued at full pace, dragging her alongside him.

"Larry, wait, I can't move that fast." Instead of slowing, he scooped her off her feet and continued to run, dragging her relentlessly behind him. Larry's grip on her arm was so tight it was cutting off her circulation. For the first time, Cleo felt true panic as she tried to yank herself free.

❧

Drake and Rock rounded the corner and ran the length of the alley. Cleo and that crazed lunatic were nowhere to be seen. They slowed briefly as they ran to check doorways and back entrances but none seemed disturbed. When they reached the end they were faced with several possibilities. The alley continued on the opposite side of the street or the two could have turned left or right. Three choices and only two of them. It would be crucial that they chose the right direction.

"Why don't we split up and loop around? I'll go this way and I'll meet you at the end of the alley."

"Wait." Drake commanded firmly. He saw something gold glinting in the sunlight on the other side of the alley. He reached down and picked up the bracelet Cleo always wore. The bracelet from her grandmother.

"They went this way." Drake pushed through a

doorway and Rock followed.

❧

Cleo had done the only thing she could think of when Larry had hesitated and entered a building. She had been trying to get a glimpse of Drake or Rock as they rounded the corner but didn't see either one as Larry pushed through the doorway, heading even further away from the restaurant.

"Larry, can't we slow down? I think we lost them." His breathing was ragged as he trudged forward and he slowed as her words began to penetrate his thoughts. "Let's just sit for a minute and talk. We can continue after I catch my breath."

Larry pushed her onto a crate in the large warehouse and stood over her, also panting for breath. "I...knew...he...was trying...to keep...you a...prisoner."

"No, he's not. Larry, I'm in love with him."

"No! You're in love with me."

She tried to console him to diffuse the situation. "Maybe under different circumstances but no. I'm not in love with you."

"But we went out. It was love at first sight."

"Not for me."

"But..."

The force that Drake used to tackle the man in front of her surprised Cleo. One second Larry was standing over her, gasping for breath and the next the two men were intertwined on the floor. Drake stood up and pulled Larry to his feet by the front of his shirt.

"Do you understand the lady's not interested?"

Larry looked at the strong man in front of him and he slowly nodded his head. "Ye..es."

"Good." Drake turned to the bouncer. "Rock,

hold this creep for me."

"With pleasure," Rock growled as he approached the short man in front of him. Larry visibly shrank as the bouncer approached, all his confidence replaced with the same insecurities Cleo had seen on their date.

Drake knelt down beside Cleo. "Are you alright?"

"Yes, now that you're here." Cleo looked from Drake to Rock, then back to Drake. "What are the two of you doing here?"

"We had planned to have lunch together and decided we wanted 'a world famous' sandwich from Nate & Al's."

"I believe that was 'best sandwiches in town'..."

"Aaah, I think you're right."

"I didn't know you two were having lunch." Cleo smiled.

Rock laughed. "I didn't want Drake to tell you until we'd had a chance to meet and work out the details."

"What details?"

Drake looked at Rock. "Do you want to tell her or should I?"

"Tell me what?"

"I'm the new intern at TSA."

Cleo squealed. "That's great!"

"But wait, there's more... My first project is working on the new Healthy Shine commercials. Cool, huh?"

Cleo laughed. "Way cool."

"So what are we going to do with this creep?" Rock stood over Larry whose body was slumped over in resignation.

"I think the police will be interested in talking

to him."

"Do you still have that portable phone with you?" Drake handed the phone over to Rock. "I'll take care of that for you right now."

"Ask for Deputy Schmidt at the sheriff's department."

"Sure thing." Rock dialed 9-1-1.

"It's that take charge kind of attitude that is going to make Rock a great intern at the agency."

"Hey, that's Henry to you, Drake. You, too, Cleo." The three laughed.

It didn't take long for a squad car to arrive. Larry was whisked away to the police station for questioning.

"What's going to happen to him?"

"Well, he's facing a variety of charges, including burglary and kidnapping. I think it's safe to say he won't be bothering you anymore."

"What a relief."

"I think you dropped something a little while ago." As Drake pulled her bracelet out of his pocket, Cleo realized she'd forgotten all about it in the commotion of the afternoon. "Good thinking. I knew exactly how to find you once I saw it." Drake slipped the gold bracelet over her wrist and fastened the clasp. A warm current shot up her arm at the physical contact between them.

Rock's voice boomed between them. "Are you guys hungry? Because I'm starving. Dealing with crazies always makes me hungry."

"Rock, you're always hungry."

"Hey, I'm a big guy. I've got to keep up my figure."

"Sure, let's go." Cleo stood up and put an arm out for each of the men at her side. "You're my heroes. Thanks for coming to the rescue."

As if on cue, both men leaned down and kissed her on each side of her cheeks.

CHAPTER ELEVEN

They chose a booth at the deli. Rock sat down across from Cleo and Drake slid into the seat next to her. For most of the meal Drake held her hand under the table. She marveled that he was able to eat his entire meal with his left hand. Rock didn't seem to notice.

Cleo laughed as she watched Rock consume a meatloaf dinner with mashed potatoes and gravy, six dinner rolls and two pieces of apple pie with vanilla ice cream. He finally leaned back and patted his stomach. "Aaah, much better."

"I'm glad you're happy."

"I always get hungry when I get scared."

"You were scared?"

"Not half as bad as Drake. You should have seen his face when you disappeared around the corner of that alley."

Drake looked uncomfortable. "I knew he was a loose cannon and I didn't know what to expect." He paused, "Are we done?"

They nodded and Drake picked up the check and headed towards the cash register, leaving Cleo and Rock at the booth. Rock leaned forward and whispered, "Drake likes to be in control. He doesn't want you to know how worried he was about you. He was uneasy about what that creep might do. That's why we came down here. He's crazy about you but he just doesn't want you to know." Rock took another bite of pie.

"Why all the secrecy, I don't know. It's obvious you two are madly in love with one another."

Cleo wanted to believe him. "Are you a psych major or something?"

"No, English Lit. But people have been writing about this stuff for years. You two read like an open book."

"Gee, thanks Rock."

"Call me Henry," he said with a smile.

৵

The three walked to the parking lot and parted ways.

"I'm going to take Rock back to the agency and then I have an errand to do. I'll see you at the house later on."

"Remember, I need to be at Podium by nine."

"I should be back home by six. I'll call Joan and let her know we need to eat early tonight."

Cleo enjoyed the drive back to Drake's house but the fantasy was about to end. She would start packing her things as soon as she got to the beach house.

The sun was just beginning to set and mauve and golden highlights glistened on the surface of the Pacific Ocean. Cleo was going to miss the view from the house. She stood for a long time, trying to memorize every shadow and hue of light so she wouldn't forget. She would treasure the memories of her time at Drake's home. For a brief glimpse she'd been able to make it her own. As much as she enjoyed the house, her real heartache was when she thought about how much she was going to miss Drake.

She gathered up her two duffle bags and carried them to the garage entrance. She placed her satchel and organizer along with the overnight bags near the door and she did a quick inventory to make sure she'd included everything. She had everything except her robe. Her robe was hanging in Drake's bathroom.

She glanced at her watch. Drake would be home any minute. She wanted to make sure she was completely packed before he arrived. She wanted him to know that she understood the arrangement had been a temporary one.

She took the stairs two at a time, wanting to get in and out of Drake's bedroom as quickly as she could. The thought of not sharing his bed later that night and for the nights to come caused her throat to restrict. She might spend the night with him in the future but it wouldn't be the same. She would be spending the night, not living there.

She folded the silk robe over her arm and headed towards the bedroom door. She saw Drake coming up the flight of stairs, loosening his tie as he walked. He looked incredible.

"Hi, honey, I'm home." Drake pulled her into his arms and kissed her thoroughly. They clung to each other, not wanting to break the spell.

Finally Drake pulled back, but didn't release her. "Why are your bags by the garage?"

"Because I'm moving back to my apartment. Wasn't that the arrangement? That I could stay here until it was safe for me to go home?"

"Originally." Drake looked thoughtful before he started to speak. "Rock was right. Seeing you today, being carried away by that lunatic, scared me to death. I don't want to lose you again. Stay with me, Cleo. Don't leave."

"Drake, sooner or later I'm going to have to leave. I have my life to live. I don't want to be tucked away here like a treasure."

Drake laughed. "I know that." He pushed his fingers through his hair. "I'm not saying what I want to say very well but I've never done this before." He took her hand in his and led her to the edge of the bed. "Sit down." She sat and he knelt down beside her.

"What I'm trying to say is..." Drake reached into his pocket and pulled out a small velvet box. "Will you marry me?"

Cleo's voice was a whisper. "What?"

Drake swallowed hard. "I love you. I don't want to lose you. Will you marry me?"

Cleo could feel tears welling up in her eyes as she flung her arms around his neck. "Yes! Drake, l love you so much. It was tearing me up inside to think of leaving."

They kissed for a long time. Finally Drake pulled back. "Do you want to see the ring? If you don't like it, we can pick one out together."

Cleo didn't care if the ring had come out of a gumball machine. Drake was what was important to her. She watched as he carefully lifted the lid and slipped the ring onto her finger. It fit her finger perfectly.

"Drake, it's beautiful." The ring was made out of platinum. A large emerald cut diamond was in the center with two triad-cut diamonds on either side. Sapphires were set flush within the band. Cleo couldn't imagine a more perfect ring.

They made love together, savoring each moment, not wanting to rush. Afterwards they lay in bed intertwined. Drake was the first one to speak. "How do you feel about long engagements?"

"I haven't really given it any thought."

"Good, because I don't want us to have one."

"Watch out or I may have to torture you again."

"Promises, promises."

Cleo kissed him and she could feel his body hardening beneath her. "Actually, I'll have to torture you later. I have to get to work."

Drake rolled over on top of her, poised between her thighs. "You're going to leave me like this?"

Cleo moaned.

"Who do you think is torturing whom?"

"Debatable. Come a little closer and I'll tell you."

Drake thrust inside her and she gripped his shoulders and they found a rhythm in their lovemaking before they climaxed together.

Cleo reluctantly untangled herself and pushed herself off the bed. "I've got to get to work. I'm going to take a quick shower." As she walked towards the bathroom the phone began to ring. It was nice not to flinch at the sound. Pavlov's dogs had been put to rest.

"Hello? Sure, hold on. Cleo, it's for you."

Cleo looked puzzled as she took the receiver

from Drake. "Hello?"

"Darling, its Raymond. You're never going to believe what just happened. The other actress that was cast to do the Meyerson film can't do it! She has other obligations during the shooting schedule. If you're free, you've got the part. Don't tell me you have plans during the next three months or I'm jumping out my office window right now."

"Raymond, your office is on the first floor."

"I know, honey, but you better be free anyway. Are you doing anything that I don't know about?"

"Well, I have the two Healthy Shine commercials..."

"Yeah, but those we can work around. Stockton seems like an agreeable sort of guy."

"Raymond, there is one other commitment I haven't told you about."

"Cleo, my heart can't take this. What is it?"

"I've got a honeymoon to take."

"My god, Cleo, when did this happen? Who is it?"

"Don't worry Raymond, my fiancé is an agreeable sort of guy. I'm sure he'll be flexible."

"Honey, are you engaged to that sexy, hunk of a man, Drake Stockton?"

"You know him?" Cleo started to giggle. "Raymond, I'll call you tomorrow."

As she hung up the phone, Drake wrapped his arms around her. "Did you get the part?"

Cleo nodded affirmation. "You're right, Drake. Tomorrow always promises to bring something better.

"With you in my life, darling, today is perfect and all of my tomorrows promise to be, too."

ABOUT THE AUTHOR

Paris Tyler has been writing most of her life and enjoys creating stories in a modern 20th century setting when life was simpler and technology hadn't intruded on personal interactions (even though she's addicted to her iPhone in the 21st century!) OTHERWISE ENGAGED, the third romantic story by Paris Tyler, will be the next book published by Love Swan Books.

ABOUT THE COVER ARTIST

Sam Mayle is a UK based freelance illustrator. He graduated from Colchester Institute with a degree in Graphic Design. He's been drawing and doodling since he could hold a pen and is influenced by sci-fi, fantasy and everyday life. He works in the London/Essex area.

Love Swan
—— Books ——

For more information about Love Swan Books, please visit www.loveswanbooks.com or email info@loveswanbooks.com.